Gloriana

by

Oliver Richbell

Novella Nostalgia

Published by City Fiction

Copyright © 2018 Oliver Richbell

ISBN: 978-1-910040-20-1

On 11th May 1812 Spencer Perceval was shot and killed.
His assassin was convicted, tried and executed seven days later.
Murder was not at that time uncommon nor is it now;
However, Spencer Perceval was 'Primus Inter Pares'.

He was The Prime Minister.

Brexit is the political equivalent of a Force 12 hurricane
and for many it is a cataclysmic disaster that has to be
stopped at any cost.

Even if that means murdering The Prime Minister.

THE CONSPIRATORS

Sir William Bretherinby
The Cabinet Secretary and the most senior
Civil Servant in the country.

Clive Ferringsly QC
A retired Lord Chief Justice and former joint-head
of the 'Remain' legal team.

Brigadier General Xavier Llewellyn-Jones
One of the most highly decorated and experienced
military figures of his generation.

Katherine MacStones
The Attorney General and Chief Legal Adviser
to the Crown.

Philip Nicholson
The Master of the Royal Household and personal
confidante to the Royal Family.

Sebastian Pennington
Permanent Secretary to the Home Office
who is responsible for law and order and security
in Great Britain.

Samantha (Sam) Wyde
Director General and Chief Economic Advisor
to the Treasury who oversees the economic and
fiscal groups in the Treasury and is co-head of the
Government Economic Service.

GLORIANA

The morning mist rose from the Thames like swirls of white candyfloss and as his jet-black chauffeur-driven car glided over Westminster Bridge, Sebastian Pennington was idly peering through the tinted windows watching the great unwashed shuffling along on the pavement.

It was not just the mist that made these daily commuters move ponderously but it was, in fact, because they were glued to the screens of their mobile phones. No-one seemed to be aware of each other as they sauntered along. Sebastian smiled as one suited gentleman dodged around a small group of tourists as they stopped mid-stride for their latest photo. It was a side-step worthy of a world class rugby player and as he dodged and swerved he broke his avid attention to his hand-held technical device to perform a superbly timed photo-bomb by jutting his head sharply upwards and to the left like some displaying meerkat.

Sebastian allowed himself an inward chuckle as he was driven past this Pythonesque moment and as he turned to look over his shoulder the man had continued walking, already head down and re-immersed with his phone.

Sebastian adjusted the wings of his Thomas Pink shirt, feeling the folds of his tie and its double-Windsor knot. He was tense and he knew it. Earlier that morning it had taken him five attempts to get his tie as he wanted; it normally only took him two but his fingers just didn't want to function as usual.

Nervous energy he concluded, so he declined his usual morning Nespresso. He also didn't want to take the risk of ruining his immaculately pressed shirt or tie.

He was now regretting not having that first hit of coffee as he could sense a gigantic yawn was coming. Like most people he lived off that powerful bean to get him going in the morning. He fought the sleepiness that he sensed was washing over him by pinching his nose hard with his right hand; it didn't work as he arched his back and yawned for Britain.

His car, a pristine Jaguar, always had a valet-fresh aroma and this mattered to Sebastian as he enjoyed all things prim, proper and refined. The sole exception to this rule was with his mistresses, who he preferred to be anything but sophisticated. The selection last night from Madame Verity, the most discreet of the co-ordinators in London, was just right for his tastes and his mood.

Whatever the woman's name was didn't matter as they were never invited to stay the night. Sebastian always preferred the middle of his bed and even when he was back home, in his Georgian cottage with his Wife, Natalie, he would insist on occupying the centre of the marital mattress.

However, as of late and by his personal preference he was rarely at home with Natalie, especially when the only thing that welcomed him there was the mat on the doorstep.

Rather than heading to Whitehall, Sebastian called out to Jonathan, "Slight detour this morning please Jonathan. Victoria Embankment if you would."

Jonathan, who had been Sebastian's driver for longer than he wanted to remember, inwardly cursed as he was hopeful of a cheeky little catnap after dropping off his charge – he always looked forward to his flick through

The Sun newspaper and then ten or so minutes shut-eye before the obligatory cleaning and valeting.

His response was however as courteous as ever, "Of course Sir" despite the fact that it meant fighting the morning traffic around Parliament Square to get onto Victoria Embankment as there was presently no right turn after Westminster Bridge. What was the point, contemplated Jonathan, about having a bigwig in the back if he couldn't flout a few road signs.

After a minute or so of driving, Jonathan glanced into his rear-view mirror to try and gauge precisely where he was meant to be going. Victoria Embankment was unusually a very vague destination; however, his normally alert and focused passenger seemed to be lost in his thoughts.

Driving around London was never easy but with a saloon Jaguar it was always slightly more precarious, certainly with the volumes of neon-clad cyclists cutting in and out of gaps in the traffic like leaping, luminous salmon. Jonathan just continued to slowly meander along waiting for his instructions.

Cruising in his Jaguar, Jonathan knew it wasn't his but he liked to tell himself that it was and it made him feel important and wealthy; after all why couldn't he daydream a little; everyone is a legend in their own bath time so why shouldn't he be? Most of the rest of his regiment who left the army around the time he did were either working as security guards at supermarkets or breaking their backs labouring, whereas he got to drive a flash motor and babysit some government toff; easy in comparison. As he carefully drove along, his mind was distracted; playing that song in his head, "He's got a brand new car, Looks like a Jaguar ..." but he couldn't for the life of him remember the name of the band.

"Stop here," came the barked order from the back seat – fortunately for Jonathan there was a sufficient break in the traffic so he was able to come to a halt on the corner of Richmond Terrace off Victoria Embankment. Jonathan looked behind him to check what he was meant to do next but he only caught sight of Sebastian's suit jacket as it was leaping out of the car which had barely slowed to a standstill. "No need to wait" came the hasty voice from Sebastian as the door slammed shut. Jonathan watched his patron stoop down to place his leather satchel between his legs so he was able to adjust his tie before marching purposely towards a rather grand looking modern building overlooking the most famous of rivers.

It was not uncommon in itself for Jonathan to be asked to return to the office alone, so hearing the impatient beeping of horns behind him and catching sight of a rather angry looking cabbie giving him a two-finger salute in his rear view mirror he placed his right foot on the accelerator. Jonathan felt the immediate power at his disposal and as he pulled the dark leather steering wheel down to his right the Jaguar leapt in front of the creeping traffic and back onto Victoria Embankment and towards Horse Guard's Avenue. As he sped away he shot a quick peak over his shoulder and saw the sign "New Scotland Yard".

Jonathan thought to himself that there must be a 'to-do' on as normally the Metropolitan Police came to Sebastian at his Whitehall offices but heading back now his attention was half on whether he was going to get any kip this morning and the other half was on trying to recall the name of that band …

Sebastian had entered the modern edifice by the time Jonathan had cried out the answer to his 'name that band' quandary. "Feeder," he exclaimed as he relaxed back into his seat with a self-satisfied bum wiggle of relief. His next stop would be forty-winks with a bit of luck.

Sebastian declined to participate in the usual formalities of signing in and going through security checks. There really was no need to be so rude about it thought the guard, just because you are the Permanent Secretary to the Home Office and one of the most powerful unelected men in the country, who is basically in charge of law and order and security throughout Britain, there's no need to be such a dick. The guard, still chewing his internal dissatisfaction like it was one of the dumplings in the staff canteen, watched Sebastian march down the hallway.

Sebastian reached his destination, then he repeated the charade of adjusting his tie for the umpteenth time that morning. The door was closed and as Sebastian placed his palm on the handle and pushed downwards he inadvertently hit his knee on the solid frame by moving forward too decisively. Letting out an audible grunt he impatiently rattled the lever expecting frustration to be the solution. After a moment or two he heard the metallic click as the door was opened from the inside.

As Sebastian entered the meeting room his attempted levity was a serious misjudgement of the atmosphere in the room; "It comes to something that you have to lock a door inside New Scotland Yard". He smiled as he spoke and scanned the faces around the room looking to share his 'amusing' quip - he was not pleased by the ashen expressions he received so he moved for the nearest chair. As he sat down he fiddled with his tie once again.

The meeting room was modern in appearance and decor but it lacked soul. One side was glazed facing a courtyard, the back and other side wall were adorned with images from the by-gone era of London policing; the majority of which were black and white photos but there was a dominating colour one which depicted The Prime Minister standing together with the Metropolitan Police Commissioner.

Sebastian had by now opened his satchel and was about to delve into it to retrieve his note pad and pen when a voice came from the other end of the table.

"We go tonight".

With the sound of those three words Sebastian lost the sensation in his right hand thereby dropping his Mont Blanc pen into the depths of his bag.

There was an audible intake of breath as those around the room became immediately aware that the time for decisive action had arrived.

Sat at the head of the table and in charge of the group was Brigadier General Xavier Llewellyn-Jones and it was he who had caused such commotion by uttering those words that seemed to hang over them all like a net of balloons on prom night. LJ commanded respect and was idolised by all that had served under him in a highly distinguished military career that had spanned over three decades and countless countries. LJ had been on active service everywhere Britain had been in the last thirty odd years; from the first Gulf War to Afghanistan, Iraq, Sierra Leone and Bosnia.

One of Brigadier General Xavier Llewellyn-Jones' most admirable characteristics was that unlike most of his fellow 'top-brass' he didn't insist on too much formality, for example he preferred to be addressed as "LJ".

"Right then everyone, let's stop fucking about and confirm we are all green for go," commanded LJ. There was no doubt that he was the leader of the conspirators and he continued with a summons similar to what you'd hear at a rugby social, "To my left".

All eyes turned to face the Director General and Chief Economic Adviser to the Treasury: Sam Wyde.

She was dressed in a bespoke tailored charcoal grey business suit as she had a tendency to prefer suits and shirts to perhaps what is considered to be more feminine attire. In her experience she felt it necessary to be more manly, hence Sam and not Samantha. Sam's attitude had paid dividends as her "call me Sam" approach had certainly helped achieve her stated goal of becoming the youngest ever Chief Economic Adviser. She was brilliant and everyone knew it and her knowledge of macroeconomics was worthy of a Nobel Prize.

Sam was ruthless though. She was like an assassin and nothing would distract her from achieving even greater power and authority. People often mistook her for arrogant but actually, and as her favourite song went, she was in reality just a 'cold hard bitch'.

Her one fault was that she was perhaps too calculating and preferred to prefix her statements with caveats or to be overly generic in her replies in order that she maintained a comfortable and balanced seat on the fence. After all, the primary rule of Whitehall was survival and the best way to survive was not to adopt a polarised position.

Sam began to speak with a calm and deliberate purpose as she carefully uttered her planned opening statement "All that has been needed to be done has been done, therefore…"

LJ was not a fan of this Whitehall rule.

"Well fuck me. What does that mean?" snapped LJ. "Any chance you could take that civil service arse-covering dictionary out of your mouth for just one minute!"

"Look here LJ," responded Sam - "There is no need for me to spell it out is there?" With an intake of breath she looked around the room and stated, "We have all spent a great deal of time getting everything in place, we know what we're doing and what is at stake. The Treasury are on board provided that events go as we have planned so let's just Leave it at that". After seeking out eye-contact with LJ she added "OK?" But for once her confidence eluded her and those two letters got stuck in her throat so she coughed into her right hand and repeated, "OK?" with a little more volume and force than before.

The room fell silent as they waited for LJ to reply and Sebastian felt that it was his job to speak so with the obligatory knot shuffle, he opened his mouth and took a deep gulp of the stale air-conditioned air. However, he had lost his moment as to the right of Sam a voice was heard which left Sebastian with his mouth agape and his right hand off the table and index finger out as if he were attempting to enter his pin code at an invisible cash point.

The voice belonged to Katherine MacStones, the Attorney General and the Chief Legal Adviser to the Crown. She was not Scottish but she had married Douglas MacStones of MacStones LLP, the largest and most influential law firm in Scotland. Katherine had been in and out of foster-homes all her childhood, not that she wanted to remember anything of her formative years. She had worked hard at college and her absolute tenacity and sheer gritty stubbornness got her through university and law school and into a decent mid-sized legal practice in Newcastle. She met her future husband at a conference and despite what was rumoured, she fell immediately in love with him.

Katherine became Katherine MacStones within a few months of their meeting, a partner not long after and managing partner a few years later. With her no-nonsense approach and 'common touch' her stock kept rising and she was elected to Parliament with a vast majority and became the Attorney General within her first elected term. However, despite every success that came her way it was never enough for Katherine as she felt that in spite of everything she was unable to rid herself of the stigma of her early life. It was irrational paranoia on her part but she couldn't help it; her only cure was to amass more and more money and power.

Katherine was, on occasion, fond of adding a little Scottish twang to her words as she spoke and this was one such occasion "As I (which came out as aye) see it, if LJ says we are on, then we are on". Accepting the nods from around the room Katherine continued, "This is it, the die is cast and if need be I'll play Brutus myself".

Sam didn't wait for her to continue as she forcefully interjected, "Look here, Katherine," she almost spat out her name, "It's all very well you being so candid about it but we are talking High Treason here, not some slap on the wrist misdemeanour and I think there needs to be some carefully chosen words".

Katherine turned to face Sam, "Tell me Samantha what exactly have you got to add right now?". The measured choice of 'Samantha' was a deliberately barbed comment designed to 'score a point' and attempt to establish an aura of dominance. Sam's reaction was, in the opinion of the men in the room, as calm as a Las Vegas poker ace but as the two women were, at best only a foot away, Katherine saw the flicker of indignation in Sam's eyes.

Katherine pressed on.

"We've been through this on more than one occasion; there are no listening devices and we've all left our mobiles and computers at work or at least disabled the tracking and recording functions." Sebastian gulped and his mouth fell open again as he tried to remember if he had disabled the tracker and microphone on his government issue smartphone.

"So, what is your problem here?" Katherine asked of Sam and the stress placed on 'your' was overly emphasised to highlight that Sam was isolating herself from the rest of the group.

Sam, sensing that the five sets of male eyes were observing this 'interchange' like sports fans watching the opening rounds of a boxing bout, reacted with gusto.

"Katherine I know you are built to play Brutus"; the dig at her weight hit home better than Brutus' dagger did as Katherine recoiled. Sam attacked again, "but there has to be some class to what we are doing here." Sam deliberately pronounced the 'we' louder than the rest of the sentence but the comment addressed to Katherine about 'class' was another knife wound and given the blazing eyes that stared back at her, Sam knew she had scored.

LJ had heard enough of the persistent sniping between Katherine and Sam – he liked them both, of course he did, but he had not counted on the personality clash between them. Clash was a polite way of describing it.

LJ resented what he perceived as the lily-livered Whitehall attitude which, in his personal opinion, had started this entire mess in the first place. He was not a fan of lawyers either, he never had been but especially not after his second wife had dragged his good name through the divorce courts using his money to pay for a bulldog of a barrister to nail him to the wall.

He was a pragmatist though and was acutely aware that the Treasury and the Attorney General's office needed to be fully onside if his plan was to succeed. It was always referred to by LJ as 'his' plan although it was certainly not his entirely. LJ had structured, formed and named The Committee and had, of course, nominated himself as Chair, but this was no ordinary cross-departmental committee that reported back up the chain of command.

The Committee was the secret kind; the top-secret kind; the kind of committee that had no minutes taken, no records of any sort and it could only meet with every member present. It was an 'all for one, one for all' quorum and although he had never read anything by Alexandre Dumas, LJ would have liked the sobriquet of one of the musketeers. Instead he settled on the slightly un-original 'LJ'.

The first meeting of The Committee had taken place in LJ's country house in the Cotswolds. It was a very informal occasion, cigars and brandy were offered and taken by some including MacStones, which LJ highly approved of, and it was agreed by all that something had to be done to prevent the United Kingdom's exit from the European Union.

Brexit, as the population as a whole knew it, was voted for by just 51.9% of the votes cast – which meant that 48.1% voted to Remain. But the staggering percentage from The Committee's point of view was that the turnout was just 72.2% of those eligible to vote. There were 27.8% of voters who didn't turn out for such a crucial decision which was more than enough to have changed the result. LJ did have to concede the point from Sebastian that not all of those who did not vote would have voted Remain; if they had all voted it could, for argument's sake have increased the Leave share of the vote. LJ accepted the notion in principle but rejected the hypothesis on the basis that the Leave Campaign had been predicated on mistruths and false promises and that if the electorate had been truthfully informed and not pandered to like cantankerous children, there was no plausible way the United Kingdom would have voted to Leave the European Union.

As the cigar smoke swirled around their heads like pirouetting ballerinas and the brandy decanter was emptied and refilled and emptied and refilled again the opinions and words from those present became more militant and radical.

It was LJ who first talked of 'taking direct action' with MacStones the first to suggest that if a change of policy was to be achieved it could not occur through typical constitutional means.

Out of a brandy-fuelled bombastic rant-athon came the kernel of an idea that it might just be possible to alter Britain's future. It was very high risk but nevertheless the conclusion LJ came to when the last of his guests had stumbled upstairs to the bedrooms was that in fact it might just be possible.

The Committee were now sat in New Scotland Yard - after all what better place to plan the assassination of The Prime Minister than one of the most secure buildings in the entire country. It was the person to MacStones' left who spoke next.

Lord Chief Justice Clive Ferringsly QC (retired) had been the Law Lord – he was respected and feared in equal measures throughout the British Legal System as not only a fierce and brilliant judicial mind, who was often the scourge of Barristers that appeared before him, but also an ardent Pro-European. He had been, some weeks before, joint-head of the Remain Campaign's legal team so what he didn't know about European Jurisprudence was in his own words "not worth a cent". It was perhaps not as widely known that his private business interests spread deep into the very fabric of the European Union from farming subsidies to industrial and telecommunication conglomerates.

Clive had known LJ for years, pre-dating the first European Referendum in 1975. They were not brothers but through the warm embrace they always met with you'd be convinced that more than just friendship bound them together.

It was now Clive's turn to speak and just as he did when he sat presiding in Court he waited until silence was all that was to be heard. "We have spent many days getting ready for today". He rolled his grey head around the room as he spoke ensuring that he made eye contact with everyone, not just to make sure all understood the severity of what they were about to undertake but also to ensure that each and every person present knew that it was his turn to 'hold Court' and that each set of ears needed to be solely focused on him.

"There is," he continued with a gravitas in his voice that only the very leading Judges possessed, "a need to be cautious" he nodded to Sam as he spoke". However, now is the time for caution to be replaced with action".

He let these last few words resonate around the sealed room. Then with even greater purpose he added, "As you all know, my role in our great endeavour is to ensure that my fellow members of the Judiciary, in conjunction with our *dear* Attorney General MacStones …". In any other situation Katherine would have forcefully interjected after such a crass and misogynistic use of 'dear'. However, she allowed her annoyance to abate as no-one else, including Sam, seemed to have picked up on the comment the way she had … "are able to advise on the appropriate legal steps necessary to reverse Article 50".

Clive was now firmly in his element and talking in ever increasing grandiose terms of 'saving Britain', 'protecting the future' and enhancing the role that they all could play in re-shaping the modern political landscape. MacStones' own personal view point was that it was the same old rhetoric that she had heard too many times before. She gave Clive the deference he needed but as she sat looking at him she felt an unease wash over her that she didn't welcome and perhaps more disturbingly couldn't dismiss.

Clive had done an outstanding job of losing the focus of The Committee. They had been called by LJ to ratify and agree the final decision that had been deliberated over for so long but by talking too much without saying a great deal LJ sensed that the tension levels of everyone were rising dangerously high.

With a curt but gentle, "I could not agree more my *dear* friend," glancing at MacStones as he spoke which elicited a flicker of a smile and appreciation from her for his careful and deliberate enunciation of 'dear'. "However," he continued, "there are a few more people from whom we need to hear". Taking the hint from his great friend but in a rather too ostentatious gesture, Clive announced by waving his right hand as if he were a conductor at the Albert Hall, that he was vacating the speaking privilege and the next member of The Committee began to speak.

Sir William Bretherinby was Cabinet Secretary, the most senior Civil Servant in the UK and a role that spanned the administrative element of Government and the elected politicians. Bretherinby was a unique individual and he was fiercely proud of that fact as, unlike so many of his predecessors, he was not educated at Oxford or Cambridge and his family was neither part of the political elite or establishment. His great grandfather had made his money in developing a hugely successful and profitable cabinet making company and his entire family had, at one stage or another, been employed by 'Bretherinby Cabinets'. It was his father who, along with several others, created the Worshipful Society of Cabinet Makers in 1951. William, however, chose a different path and joined the Civil Service straight from Grammar School and now as the nation's most senior of Civil Servants, the coincidence was not lost on him that whilst Bretherinby Cabinets continued to prosper, he himself was Cabinet Secretary.

Sir William, as he preferred to be addressed, surveyed the room and mused that The Prime Minister's own Cabinet meetings were seldom so proactively attended. "LJ, as ever you defer too much to me". With an exchange of nods, Sir William continued, "The PM's nominated Deputy is ready and has the necessary backing; but we are all in dark and uncharted waters".

A murmur of appreciative noises came from around the table.

"Negotiations with the EU have stalled and we are firmly on the back foot not least because there is utter confusion in the Government as to what the actual strategy and final deal is to be. Transitional Brexit is an ill-judged political folly as we cannot afford to pay the settlement demanded now or indeed in the future.

More but louder mutterings echoed around the room. There was a rap of knuckles to Sir William's left as Philip Nicholson, the Master of the Royal Household displayed his utter agreement for the words he had just heard.

Sir William after a careful and perceptive scan of those present resumed. "The change therefore, that will be achieved by our deeds this day will be remembered for all eternity. So, let us all be very clear". With a cough to clear his throat ready for the big finale Sir William decreed, "The Brexiteers must be eliminated and a change must be made but that in itself is not enough. Permanently removing The PM is the only way".

With that he stopped talking and deferentially nodded at LJ.

LJ had winced when Sir William mentioned 'Brexiteers' and he was glad he'd stuck with the moniker of LJ rather than adopting one of the names of Dumas' Musketeers for this great endeavour.

Sir William then turned to Philip Nicholson who retorted to his remarks with a perfectly delivered, "Well you've certainly had your vitamins this morning," and with a wide toothy smile, Philip then addressed his fellow conspirators.

"The Royal Household cannot intervene in the political decision making process regardless of how ruinous such policies may be". He hesitated slightly, "but I am assured that if all goes to plan a new government will be invited to the Palace by this time tomorrow". Philip sat back in his chair to indicate that he had nothing further to say.

All eyes then turned on Sebastian.

After a few moments of excruciating silence, LJ broke the stillness with a verbal sledgehammer. "For fucks sake, Sebastian. This is not the time for you, of all people, to lose the power of speech!"

Sebastian smiled weakly and with an overtly uncomfortable squirm he looked down the table at LJ.

"The Trade Delegation has arrived and the reception is set for nineteen hundred hours at Number 10". LJ appreciated the use of the military timing.

"We all have the authority to lead our respective departments and divisions to the outcome that we have agreed is best for Britain and as soon as it is done I will confirm to you, LJ, that '*Gloriana*' needs to be put into immediate action".

With that Sebastian reached for his bag and unlike his now permanently lost Mont Blanc pen he was able to retrieve a crisp manila envelope which was emblazoned with the stamp, MOST SECRET.

With as much showmanship as he could muster Sebastian spun the folder on the desk and tried to slide it down to the far end like he was a barman in a wild-west saloon.

It would have been quite the dramatic moment if it had worked. Instead the folder failed to glide more than a quarter of its intended journey so Sebastian rose and reached out over the table to claw it back and also to try and regain control of the situation. The folder was just out of his reach though and his fingers only just managed to touch it resulting in actually moving the envelope slightly further away.

Katherine, correctly sensing Sebastian's need for help to end this comical interlude, leant forward and with absolutely no panache whatsoever she gruffly shunted the paperwork into the waiting clutches of LJ.

LJ ripped the envelope open with the care of a child on Christmas morning and delved straight in as he rapidly thumbed the pages, nodding his approval as he did so. He smiled as he saw the signature of The Prime Minister at the bottom of the final page. Closing the envelope he placed the package back onto the table and planted his index finger of his right hand down onto it as if he was expecting a gust of wind to blow it away.

He addressed The Committee.

"Well done Sebastian," he boomed. Sebastian's shoulders pushed back arrogantly against the seams of his suit jacket. "What we have here my friends is '*Gloriana*', a governmental policy document about what will happen in the event of the assassination of The Prime Minister". Pausing for effect and scanning the room with his keen eagle-eyes, LJ continued. "*Gloriana* sets out that given the constant increased terrorist threat it has become necessary to plan for the 'what if' scenario." The other members of The Committee were sat in anticipatory apprehension and were silently immersed in LJ's words. This was save for Sebastian who, whilst hearing LJ, was inwardly pondering whether Catesby, Wright, Wintour, Percy et al had had a similar sense of fear and excitement on 5 November 1605 as they moved to destroy the House of Lords with gunpowder. A sudden and excruciatingly painful thought flashed across Sebastian's mind. With furtive unease his pupils shot from left to right and right to left, his hands clammed up and he could feel his brow becoming moist with sweat. He felt as if he were going to faint as he roughly grabbed his tie and pulled it down to open the gateway to his lungs; If LJ, as their leader, was Robert Catesby, did that make him Guy Fawkes?

"Sebastian," LJ's voice got louder. "Sebastian!"

Sebastian stared down the length of the table and realised that he had not only lost his poise and demeanour but he hadn't the faintest clue what LJ had been saying for the last minute or so.

"You OK my dear chap?" asked LJ. These paternalistic warming words eased Sebastian's nerves and he mumbled, "I'm fine, I just find these damn sealed coffins unbearable". He reached for the water and took a deep noisy swig of his topped-up glass. He sat down and adjusted back his tie which LJ took as a sign that he could move on.

"*Gloriana* now, with the careful amendments overseen by our talented Mr Pennington," with that murmurs of appreciation tumbled towards Sebastian and of course he accepted them all as if he were on stage collecting an Oscar, "details that if a PM is assassinated then the successor can take any swift, decisive action that they see fit. Moreover," continued LJ, "the succeeding Prime Minister has also been afforded extensive special and unilateral further powers. We have also accepted that the heir-apparent is the Chancellor of the Exchequer and whilst as unpalatable as that might appear, the long-term success of our great endeavour is the eradication of both these disastrous people".

With a slight gap to take a hushed breath LJ followed on with, "As we know, my esteemed friends ..." he opened his arms like some semi-Vitruvian man in an effort to 'air-embrace' everyone around the table "… policies can be reversed and decisions untaken provided that the leadership has the authority to lead".

"Now with the re-written *Gloriana* policy we have it".

LJ smiled once again towards Sebastian and, with his previous embarrassments forgotten, he now had the attention that he craved, and sat motionless basking in the spotlight that was now firmly shone upon him and for those brief moments he forgot his comparisons to the Gunpowder Plot conspirators.

After he re-adjusted his tie, Sebastian moved his empty glass of water to one side so he could place his elbows commandingly down in front of him.

In a poor imitation of LJ's earlier words, Sebastian began with, "What we have here," but he immediately realised that he was no LJ and more overtly the *Gloriana* paper he wanted to refer to was still at the other end of the table.

LJ took this as his cue to return their crucial manuscript and with a graceful indifference he spun the folder expertly and precisely down the table towards Sebastian. It neither lifted nor collided with the half emptied water jug or any of the glasses. The folder rotated as if on an axis and glided beautifully to a rest between Sebastian's elbows; it even finished up with the embossed MOST SECRET mark perfectly positioned at Sebastian's eye level. Clive and LJ shared a smile together as Clive winked his approval at his friend for a perfect piece of showmanship. There was no doubt that LJ possessed the requisite authority to lead.

Sebastian recounted, with accurate detail how his position, and his position alone, enabled him to carefully and discreetly restructure *Gloriana* into what The Committee required. There were no fundamental shifts of seismic proportions but a series of tweaks and rephrases that ever so neatly enabled any subsequent Prime Minister to assume almost ultimate influence in the event of a fatal terror attack on the office of *Primus Inter Pares*. Parliament had previously voted, almost unanimously, to provide, if needed, the nation's leader with the authority to assume a level of power necessary to deal with imminent and real threats to the United Kingdom. It was also decreed that such powers were transferable onto successors of the then Prime Minister in the event and as *Gloriana* subtly stated, "there was forced upon Her Majesty's Government an abrupt change in leadership".

Sebastian proceeded to illustrate how he had been able to construct the appropriate influence over The Prime Minister's staff and aides in his capacity as Permanent Secretary to the Home Office so he was able to provide documents for signature without the obligatory review and analysis. The Prime Minister approved of the title – assuming it was a reference to the Royal Rowbarge – and signed it without as much as a cursory scan of the contents.

Sebastian had been 'holding Court' for some considerable time and yet no-one interrupted him; there were not even any assenting words or sounds. For the first time since The Committee was formed, Sebastian truly felt important, and this mattered to him. It mattered a great deal.

However, he overplayed his hand as he then declared, "So let me recap".

LJ pounced.

He had waited long enough but knowing that feeling important was important to Sebastian he had allowed him his moment in the spotlight, but LJ was conscious that the meeting had been a long one and it would not help their cause one iota if questions were asked as to where everyone had been for the last few hours.

"No need Sebastian," said LJ in a firm but fair way. "You have done us and your country proud". He paused and, sensing it would be important to Sebastian, he added, "and I am sure that shortly we all will congratulate you on such a fine and complete application of your duties". With that LJ started a slow but steady round of applause which, albeit mutedly, was followed by every other member of The Committee. MacStones even nodded her approval towards Sebastian.

Sebastian accepted this acclaim in a less than gracious way. Sam felt he did so in a way that resembled a student actor thinking he had just performed at the National Theatre after actually just having subjected a partial audience to an insufferable amateurish performance of Hamlet.

LJ waited a moment or two to allow the reverberations of the subdued applause to evaporate. It didn't take too long.

"Well then everyone," he commenced, "we are now at the precipice and we must decide if our great endeavour is to be accomplished or are we, like so many groups before, just full of hot air".

With that he turned to Sam who was ready to be more definitive with her words. It was not lost on her that she had enjoyed a meteoric rise by not adopting polarised positions but she was certain that The Committee would succeed and so was desperate not to be on the outside looking in. She was vehemently opposed to Brexit and despite her obvious talents could not make any lasting economic argument to support the Leaving of the EU. Her job was to lead the Government's economic strategy. Yet there was none, not a shred of detail that was capable of sustaining her brilliant analysis. She concluded therefore that Great Britain needed to Remain.

So with confidence she declared, "None of my senior colleagues at The Treasury have any faith whatsoever in the Chancellor or The PM, they are both ostensibly making it up on a daily basis and there is a complete lack of cohesion and consistency. We therefore have no choice". It was a very polarised position to adopt but with The Committee around her there was nothing else to be said.

Sam turned to MacStones and with a waft of her jewellery free right hand she motioned Katherine to speak.

Katherine accepted this silent invitation with her usual charm "Er … OK … thanks …" She directed her next words straight into the very soul of LJ with the forcefulness of a howitzer.

"To act is treason but failing to act is worse. Everything is ready and everything must be done so that we may succeed."

With that she calmly placed her bejewelled hands on top of each other and onto the immaculately varnished table to symbolise that she had made up her mind and that there was nothing more to be said.

"Agreed," affirmed LJ.

Clive Ferringsly accepted the invisible baton from MacStones and sensing those around the room were anxious to depart and be about their business, he astutely elected to keep his comments to a minimum.

"We have acutely calculated everything. The time is upon us and we now need to act and to deliver".

With an appreciative nod from LJ, Clive could not resist one more sentence, "I'd like to also say that we have amongst us here some of the finest minds in the country and have been expertly led on our great endeavour by LJ." His words were swamped as an impromptu noise of clenched fists drumming on the table erupted.

LJ held his hands up in acknowledgement and his smile was as wide as the river that flowed just a few hundred metres from where he sat.

Sebastian joined in of course, he never wanted to be left out of anything, but he did so with more than a hint of jealousy as his earlier ovation was all but silent compared to the raucous cacophony reserved for LJ.

Sir William Bretherinby allowed the pounding din to cease before he took his turn to speak. He did so, as ever, with carefully chosen words. "Clive, you always have the innate knack of expressing yourself in such a perfect fashion," He hesitated and then continued, "I have nothing else to add, save for good luck to us all".

The last sentence was quite an odd one and made a few around the room feel more than a little uneasy. No-one had ever said 'good luck' or anything even remotely similar. After all there was no need as everything had been planned to the most exacting detail. There was neither necessity nor capacity for luck as that hinted at an element that had not been properly thought through and analysed.

LJ stepped in sensing that the tension had again risen a notch or two and with calming hands directed Philip Nicholson to speak. He did so in the measured and assured way that one would expect from The Master of the Royal Household. He confirmed that having heard from the others around the room that today was the day of action. LJ always thought that his manner and tone were too prim and proper and that Nicholson would prefer to listen than to lead. He was however an invaluable member of The Committee and its objective could not be achieved without him.

LJ had the final words.

"Tonight, we save our country and tomorrow we heal the wounds of division".

"There is nothing left to say but plenty left to do." He paused and smiled at everyone with genuine paternal affection and added, "so go to it".

That was the signal for the meeting to adjourn, chairs were moved back and everyone rose to their feet. Sebastian was first to the room entrance and saving further embarrassment he unlocked it before he tried to open the door.

All of this occurred in silence; not one word was spoken as The Committee made their separate ways out of the building. No-one signed out at reception and they spilt out onto Victoria Embankment and headed in their different directions.

It was 12:42 and just a mere six hours and eighteen minutes before the official start of the Trade Delegation reception at Number 10.

Sebastian crossed the road and wondered where Jonathan was. He scanned left and right looking for his Jaguar and began to get frustrated by the fact that his driver was not waiting for him. He delved into his satchel to locate his mobile phone but finding his Mont Blanc pen instead, he placed it, with a slight sense of relief, into his left jacket pocket. Returning to his bag he eventually found his phone underneath the copy of *Gloriana* he and The Committee had been discussing only a few moments before.

He looked down at the blank black screen and felt immediately relieved that he had turned it off. His right thumb hovered above the power button but instead he recalled his earlier instruction to Jonathan so hunkering down against the wind blowing up from the Thames he turned to walk the short journey back to his office.

Sebastian was a fast walker. He tended to pound the streets as he strode with little care or attention for his shoes, so it was only a few minutes before he reached his offices. No-one at the Home Office would ever dare to question where he had been or not been; after all he was Permanent Secretary.

Back at his desk, computer screen emitting its artificial glow and the chime of incoming e-mails incessantly announcing their arrival, Sebastian was sat rigidly in his chair staring fixedly ahead. The only indication that he was not in a trance like state was his right hand that was drumming those slender fingers on his mahogany wooden desk in a relentless rhythmic rattle.

Sebastian's afternoon was spent in a constant battle not to 'clock watch' but he couldn't help himself. A late lunch was taken in a blur at the dining hall reserved for senior Civil Servants. He later could not recall what he had to eat nor what was the major point of discussion around the table. The subject was undoubtedly 'Brexit' but the details eluded him.

He attended his scheduled afternoon meetings which, again, were dominated by the UK's exit from the European Union. As a Civil Servant, and one of the most senior ones at that, he was prohibited from deciding national policy; 'The Service' was responsible for implementing Governmental decisions and its legislative programme.

The major problem with such a responsibility placed on the entire Civil Service, and not just the department that fell under Sebastian's remit, was that the government of the day lacked a clear direction and any form or plan of a negotiation strategy. Sebastian, like so many others, was utterly shocked at the referendum result that the United Kingdom had chosen to Leave the European Union. He elected, however, not to vote as he wished to adhere to the Civil Service Code of political impartiality, but the truly petrifying situation was that this once Great Britain had decided to undertake a course of action with next to no contemplation of how to actually do it.

Sebastian was utterly convinced that if the Leave Campaign had not brazenly pledged jingoistic promises to the masses then the result could have been different. 'Could' was the best they had though and the best they had did not inspire confidence. Sebastian watched at first hand and with horror as Britain's negotiation strategy turned to meekly seeking to grab a positive sound bite or two for that day's press coverage rather than actively attempting to agree an acceptable exit deal.

From the very inner sanctum of British power Sebastian understood how ill-equipped and under prepared those leading the Brexit negotiations were. It was akin to watching the England football team in a major tournament; all promise and possibility but when the big games came there was a lack of ability to bring the trophy home. Sebastian sat idle in his chair, he could not concentrate on anything other than the time and after what felt like hours it was time for him to prepare for the Trade Delegation reception at Number 10.

He briefly and indifferently scanned his email inbox on his computer making sure that there was nothing urgent he should have dealt with. There was nothing of note.

He rose and headed towards the Gentlemen's locker room.

Walking down the long narrow corridors he became lost in his thoughts about that night's events and he truly hoped that he would not let LJ down.

LJ and Sebastian had spoken after The Committee had met. The call was via a secure government line and it was not unusual for Sebastian to spend most of his day engaged on such conversations.

LJ had come with the ingenious and blameless way of achieving "that abrupt change in leadership".

When LJ explained this a few weeks before, Sebastian had failed to grasp how it would even work let alone be successful. However LJ calmly and persuasively set out that the key component of their great endeavour was that the death of The Prime Minister could not be blamed on them or the wider disaffected groups that wanted to Remain within the European Union.

The plan to assassinate The Prime Minister was crudely simple and would take advantage of the increased and permanent heightened level of terrorist threat.

The impression that shrouded the British Parliament and its leadership in the weeks, months and years after the Referendum was one of abject disappointment. Those that voted to Leave were disappointed at the interminable delays and false promises and those that wanted to Remain were disillusioned in the failure to achieve meaningful headway with trade deals from around the world and to depart the European Union with a fair deal.

This shared disappointment and disillusionment

actually brought together both warring factions but both sides refused to acknowledge that they were actually in the same sinking boat.

LJ encapsulated these feelings of disappointment and resentment and had led The Committee to agree to his suggestion.

The bomb was set to explode shortly before the signing of the Trade Agreement. As LJ explained that it would annihilate any further extensive international trade deals and the current Prime Minister who was intent on following through on the catastrophic policy of Leaving the European Union. Lastly it would also galvanise popular support for any successor and with no alternative left other than to face the prospect of naked isolation in the face of global terrorism, whilst shackled with a crippled and dying economy, the only solution would be to reverse Article 50 and to re-join the safety and familiarity of their erstwhile European family.

The headline that morning in *The Metro* newspaper read "Trade Deal fiasco" and almost every news channel, newspaper and online political blog were lambasting The Prime Minister's efforts in trying to force through trade deals that were being driven by short-term political expediency rather than achieving lasting economic stability and growth.

LJ was now sat snuggly in a leather wing-backed chair in the bowels of his London Club reading *The Times* newspaper with gleeful interest in how events could not be working out any better for him, The Committee and their great endeavour.

As he reached for his cut crystal glass which contained the remnants of his Campari and Soda he felt pleasantly warm and comforted that all was going to plan. He rattled the ice cubes in his drink in a vain hope that he'd find more of that precious liqueur; he was disappointed.

"Another Campari and Soda, Sir," asked the deferential waiter who had heard the unmistaken call for more.

"Yes," was the single and curt reply from LJ. He held the glass out over the chair with his right hand and waited for it to be taken away and replaced, not refilled.

Sebastian meanwhile was not enjoying the same comforts. The facilities in the Gentlemen's changing room were sparse at best. One working shower cubicle, a small bench, one toilet, a urinal and two sinks. It was always cold and Sebastian regretted having to change here but it had been decreed that formal evening wear was required. Convention used to be lounge suits and/or national dress but given that the vast majority of tonight's gathering was from the Middle East it had been decided that black tie was the order of the day.

Sebastian carefully placed his Oxford shoes on the changing room floor. He loved them, especially because they gleamed and sparkled even in the dull and oppressive glow from the strip lighting above him.

He showered, dried himself and began to dress with a purpose and a composure that surprised him. He felt almost like he did on the day of his marriage. He looked at the wedding band on his left hand and felt a pang of remorse for how terribly that arrangement had descended into silent unhappiness.

Standing there with a towel around his waist and his dress shirt on but unbuttoned, he heard the door open behind him.

Arthur Easterby, Deputy Director for the Department of Defence, walked in and with the grace and political correctness you'd expect from a drunken stag party he blurted out "Nice towel, Pennington. Do you drop it as quick as you lot drop the ball over letting convicted terrorists stay in the UK?"

Sebastian spun round and launched a verbal tirade that was akin to a thousand cannons simultaneously firing their murderous salvo.

"Look here, Easterby" he spat out the name like it was poison. "You really are an odious bottom feeding little shit aren't you. You've not even removed that foul mouth of yours from your Minister's teat in two fucking years".

Sebastian hadn't noticed, or perhaps he didn't care, that his towel had fallen to his feet. He was stood wearing nothing except a loose shirt and a wedding ring as he continued on with his character assassination; "If you want to come and spend a day in my shoes rather than snivelling and scrambling around the scraps on the floor you are more than welcome". Sebastian had not appreciated that both of his sets of shoes were placed heel first towards Easterby and directly between them so the analogy, albeit unintended, was perfectly delivered.

Easterby caught sight of Sebastian's shoes but he was so taken aback by the startling and unexpected onslaught that he interjected tamely "OK … OK, Sebastian, … I think I'll let you be". He backed towards the door with his head firmly lowered to the floor.

He turned and made a hasty exit but not before he heard, "Fuck off you prick!" from a raging Sebastian whose blood was up and his heart rate was pounding as adrenalin pumped through his body.

Sebastian was very impressed with himself and how he had confronted Easterby head-on as he would normally bait him for hours. Today, however, was a different day and it was going to be Sebastian's day. He was also satisfyingly delighted to notice as he looked down that it was not just his blood that was up.

Sir William was neither enjoying the delights of a Campari and Soda nor the heady euphoria of standing up to an adversary. He was pacing the corridors of Number 10 fussing over the details of the Trade Delegation's imminent arrival.

Bretherinby Cabinets was fixated by ensuring that even the smallest of details were cared for and addressed. Although Sir William had long left that world behind him, some habits were tough to break. He was stood in the Pillared State Drawing Room staring up at the portrait of Queen Elizabeth I which hung above the fireplace. He ran his fingers, like some inspecting matron, over the mantelpiece; he rubbed his thumb and forefingers together but could not feel or see any dust or dirt. He turned and gazed down at the massive Persian carpet that decked almost the entire floor and Sir William hoped that no-one would get entangled later on with discussing the room's fixtures and fittings. It was, after all, probably not very diplomatic nor conducive to forging trade deals to refer to anything that conjures up references to Britain's imperial history.

Sir William was distracting himself and he knew it. These delegations and meetings were not last minute affairs organised in a hurry like a boys' night out on WhatsApp. Many months had been taken up with careful and deliberate planning and pre-agreements; even the *canapés* had been chosen with the most diligent of attention. The event would, of course, be a 'dry' one to exhibit dutiful respect to specific guests of the Middle

East Trade Delegation, although Sir William knew full well that some of the British attendees would be sneaking outside for a quick hit of alcohol. At the thought of this Sir William could not hold back a wry smile as he recalled the comical episode of *Yes, Minister* where the fictional politician, Jim Hacker, excused himself on regular occasions throughout a booze-free formal reception for 'messages'. He hoped that no-one this evening would try a similar tactic and receive messages from 'Mr Smirnoff' at the Russian Embassy.

After a final detailed survey of the room Sir William closed the door behind him and motioned to those outside that the preparations had met his exacting standards. There was a huge sigh of relief from the mingling hordes as it was far from unknown for Sir William to re-start the entire arrangements simply because there was a smear on a mirror or a fleck of dirt on the floor.

If truth be told, Sir William had more pressing things occupying his mind but he understood, as LJ had dictated to him, that all needed to appear as normal as possible.

On his way past some of the preparatory team Sir William halted mid-stride to publicly chastise one of them for a thread of cotton that had protruded out of a button. "Standards," was the only word he delivered with a cold steel-like sternness. As he marched away he left the assembled cluster in no doubt who was in charge.

In her office, surrounded by her assorted underlings, Katherine MacStones was hard at work organising the seemingly never ending legal issues that Brexit had produced. Even on her busiest days at MacStones LLP she was never as swamped as she was right now. It wasn't the fact that the volume of work she needed to attend to was unmanageable it was just that there was no real clear solution or process to follow. It was an accepted legal doctrine that European Law took precedence over that of the UK, or the law of any member state come to think of it. However, post-Brexit there was a genuine confusion as to what would occur next and how the United Kingdom was going to unravel over forty years of compulsory case law, directives and regulations. Whilst at Law School she became a devotee of Lord Denning, a famous Judge, who remarked in 1974, just two years after the UK signed the Treaty of Accession to join the European Economic Community, "The Treaty is like an incoming tide. It flows into the estuaries and up the rivers. It cannot be held back".

Law School was a very faint and distant memory but those words had resonated with Katherine and she never forgot them. She sat behind her desk surrounded by documents, bundles and boxes; she felt dominated by paper as it seemed to cover every inch of space in her office. There was a rap of knuckles on her closed door and in came another sack barrow stacked with more boxes. Its supplier was a fresh-faced aide who looked pleadingly to Katherine to tell him where to drop off the latest load. Katherine waved him in and to the young man's eager delight he noticed a few spare inches of carpet in front of him, he dutifully unpacked his cargo and muttered something about bringing in the next tranche. Katherine didn't hear him but if she had her reaction would have been a deep and heavy sigh.

She had already turned her attention back to the two heads in front of her, only their heads were clearly visible as the paper mountains in front of her made it appear she'd been building a castle.

However before Katherine was able to continue there was a commotion as the aide had just noticed a fundamental flaw with his drop-off point. The reason for the spare section of carpet was because that was where the door opened so he was trying to carefully extricate himself and his trusty supply steed through the tiniest of exits. With a grunt and a shove, he was through the opening and out but not before he had opened the door a smidgen too far and had caused a domino effect of tumbling paper stacks. Boxes piled high fell into one another across the room sending streams of once collated paperwork sprawling and falling in every direction; it was as if a river of paper had burst its banks before her very eyes. With a weary groan, she recalled once again Lord Denning's words.

Katherine was an enthusiastic member of The Committee as she had been vocal, albeit behind closed doors, about The Prime Minister and the efforts taken to negotiate terms of the United Kingdom's exit from the European Union. She first met LJ at a society gathering not too long after being appointed Attorney General and Katherine was startled at how well informed he was about her career, her ambitions and even her personal political views.

They met randomly but quite frequently after that, it was almost as if LJ knew exactly where she was and when she'd be free for a quiet chat. It was after a rather sumptuous and boozy dining experience at one of LJ's many clubs that he directly launched into his crusade to 'Remain'. He was unashamedly candid in what was being contemplated by him and a few select but influential others. "We cannot allow The Prime Minister to lead us all over the cliff edge like lemmings," he declared.

Katherine never regarded herself as radical but she became more and more focused on removing The Prime Minister by any means necessary. This didn't scare Katherine, she was actually excited by it and the prospect of greater eminence tantalised even more. LJ had played the Attorney General expertly. Unlike other members of The Committee money was not that important for Katherine; it was power and fame that she craved. LJ understood that without the Chief Legal Adviser to The Crown being a willing party to their great endeavour there was a vital element missing, so she had been wooed and courted delicately but regularly and with just enough ostentatious sycophancy to gain her valuable participation.

Katherine was staring blankly ahead as the young aide and her two colleagues stared at her waiting for the eruption they fully expected. No such eruption occurred; she just slumped her head forward and let out a guttural sigh that seemed to last until every last drop of breath had been expelled from her lungs. With her head down Katherine lifted up the right sleeve on her shirt and looked at her Cartier watch – the time was 15:54.

Despite the sheer chaos around her the only thought that came to mind was "just over three hours to go".

Sam was looking forward to being back in her office but presently she was enjoying a very pleasant walk across Parliament Street and down King Charles Street. She even managed to forget her role on The Committee and the detestable 'great endeavour' that LJ insisted on calling it as she sauntered along some of London's most iconic landmarks.

Although Sam had never served in the military - she

didn't have the stomach for it - as a mark of respect she always stopped at the Cenotaph when her journey took her past.

Normally she would feel some degree of emotional connection but that day there was none. What she did feel though was a sensation that she was unable to accurately describe; it felt like sadness but it was darker than that. This feeling stayed with her for the rest of the afternoon until shortly before she departed for Downing Street and the Trade Delegation at which point she realised exactly what it was; fear.

Philip Nicholson had a secret, if anyone at the Royal Household were to find out it would personally disgrace him and certainly put some serious doubts into the minds of those that he looked after and genuinely loved. As secrets go it was nothing serious nor salacious but he wouldn't want to admit to it since his position of overall responsibility for the running of the Royal Household meant he needed to live a life beyond reproach; much like those he oversaw the care of.

Philip Nicholson of the Royal Household was a gambler. He didn't indulge in the 'sport of Kings' as perhaps some would have assumed; he didn't understand horse racing at all. It was fruit machines. But not the ones that populate the pubs and bars of London's great metropolis but those 'high-stake' machines that can only be found in betting shops or casinos.

He loved doing it, he really did love it and everything about it from the ambiance, the social dichotomy of those that frequented the 'bookies' and the buzz that would flow through his veins when he hit the jackpot. He would never openly admit it but he was utterly addicted to those flashing lights and was entirely sucked in by the names like 'A King's Ransom' or 'Emperor Reels'. Philip knew he had a problem but he justified not doing anything about it as he was, just, able to resist the temptations of playing those machines every day.

He had convinced himself that he didn't need 'it' regularly like perhaps someone with a drug or alcohol dependency who had to have their daily hit but as he sat listening to LJ and the rest of The Committee a thought – a marvellous one – occurred to him. On his journey back to Buckingham Palace he could just pop in to one of his favourite spots. Philip never just called in, even though he tried to delude himself that he did.

He was required back at Buckingham Palace in order to facilitate the final details for attendance at the Trade Delegation later that evening but he knew he could spare half an hour or so.

An hour and a half since he departed The Committee he was still sat on a faux-leather stool mechanically pressing the 'Start' button with ever increasing frustration.

In order to falsely persuade his inner-self that he was in control he never kept a running total of his 'investment' but the soon to be empty wallet would tell him he had gambled away nearly £500. There was something prophetically absurd about feeding £20 pound notes that contained the image of his employer into a machine. On particularly unlucky days, of which this was one, he would talk to the notes as they disappeared into the depths of the automated gambling machine asking it for good luck.

As he reached inside his suit jacket for the umpteenth time that afternoon and removed his hand stitched leather wallet he recoiled on his chair as he only had one note left – a rather tatty £20. There was nothing left of the £500 he had left his home with at the start of the day.

Philip could sense that others in the bookmakers were awaiting his departure in order that they could jump into his seat and chase his money. He pressed 'Start' with a little more care and delay than before to gauge the mood of the bodies he could feel were watching him and the oscillating dials on the screen in front of him.

The assembled rag-tag bunch of pasty-faced gamblers were itching for their turn. However, they were to be disappointed as with an exclamation of "finally!" the machine lit up and rang out the computerised alarm of a Jackpot. The reels sparkled and danced as the jackpot images of gold crowns on his favourite game - 'A King's Ransom' - told everyone who was in attendance that he had won big. Philip had achieved the maximum prize of £500 and with the £12 left as credit he was up. He collected his winning ticket and slithered off his perch and moved head down, to avoid unwanted eye-contact, to the counter.

He stepped out back into the world with the relieved gamblers satisfaction of basically breaking even but was astonished to see that he had been inside, cut off from reality and common sense, for just under two hours. He was now running a little late and hailed the nearest black cab to take him back to the Palace side entrance on Buckingham Gate.

The cab cost him £15 with tip.

The West End final edition of *The Evening Standard* led with 'PM pleads with Delegation' in its distinctive standard typeface. The paper contained little other stories of note and it was certainly the day to 'send out the rubbish' and release unpalatable or unpopular stories or news items. Even the back page announcing that the English Premier League had created the first million pound a week footballer didn't seem to be attracting the attention that it would have usually. After all when the lead article is talking trillions what impact would only millions have?

Clive Ferringsly had not been invited to the Trade Delegation and so he had meandered his way back to the Strand and he was hopeful of an afternoon glass or two with one of his former Barrister colleagues. He was not fussed who he drank with but he detested drinking alone; he always remarked that such an action was the precursor to whisky on your morning cornflakes.

Prior to Clive joining the judicial bench he was a well-regarded and experienced Barrister from a central London set called Hartington Chambers. As he walked through that all too familiar reception area he was greeted by all and sundry like a returning war-hero. The Barristers' clerks stood and applauded and the Head of Chambers, Rufus Herrington-Jones, bounded to embrace his mentor like a child runs to Father Christmas.

After the perfunctory platitudes Clive and Rufus were engaged in catching up over a very passable bottle of Malbec in one of the many back-street public houses that served the insatiable demand for alcohol from England's legal elite.

As the second bottle was ordered and added to the Chambers' tab, Rufus finally managed to ask Clive, "So what have you been up to?"

'If only you knew' was Clive's instinctive internal reply. Instead he responded with the banal, "Surviving my dear chap … surviving".

With that the two of them delved back into their trips down memory lane and Clive was delighted that he had a distraction from the thoughts inside his head.

As was customary the invited attendees at Trade Delegations didn't arrive *en masse* like a surprise birthday party. The majority had arrived in well-orchestrated groups in advance of the seven o'clock formal welcome speeches. The Civil Servants and representatives of the Middle East nations had been ushered solemnly into Number 10 Downing Street's Pillared State Drawing Room and were quietly making polite chit-chat awaiting the dignitaries and industry leaders.

Several high-profile business people had also been invited, most of whom were now more celebrities than true commerce professionals. But the PR teams from Number 10 had recommended that such luminaries attend to try and give the 'wow' factor to the evening. The simple logic applied was 'after all if the glitterati and celebs off the telly are in favour why should the general public not support the final deal'. The naïve reality was that the final deal was so heavily one-sided and weighted against Great Britain that it would be difficult to hide the onerous terms even if the England Football Captain explained it using his terminology: 'It's a game of two halves and we've got to keep it tight at the back and hope we can nick a draw and get a point so that we can build on that for the rest of the campaign'. No number of celebrities could gloss over the terms of the Trade Deal but The Prime Minister had made it clear that the deal had to be done. Therefore laying out the red carpet so the press could focus on the Middle East delegation rubbing shoulders with film stars and musicians was a price worth paying to get the deal 'over the line'.

Of course LJ shunned the dress code of black tie and instead had opted for his full dress uniform. He resembled a strutting peacock but in a matter of minutes he would have a great deal to swagger about. Katherine arrived looking rather ravishing in a full black evening gown and he nodded his approval as she caught his eye as she made her way into the room pausing only slightly to acquire a glass of fresh apple juice; made from English apples of course.

Sir William Bretherinby had not really settled all day but he was standing on the immaculately cleaned Persian carpet trying to engage a number of senior representatives from one of the Arab states in a casual conversation about the historical artefacts that surrounded him. Sir William was carefully focusing attention on the paintings around the room and not on the floor coverings.

Sebastian was fussing over his bow-tie as he and Sam were being lectured to by one of the celebrity business people now present about how their personal involvement and phone calls with The Prime Minister had been so crucial in achieving the deal that was about to be signed. Sebastian could not stomach much more of this self-opinionated tosh which oozed out of the mouth of someone who was only here this evening because they owned a media company which had been bequeathed to them by their father. Sam stood, appearing to be listening intently, whilst actually wondering if Sebastian had realised that his bow-tie was askew.

Philip Nicholson arrived into the chamber which predicated a hushed expectancy as necks were craned to see if the Prince of Wales had also entered the room.

In fact it was the The Prime Minister that walked in - surrounded by aides and no security. Warm handshakes were shared with the heads of the major Middle Eastern families. After a brief moment of political unease as hands were offered and not immediately taken, the room parted as if it had been choreographed, creating a greeting line for the Prince of Wales to glad-hand fellow royalty and celebrities. This signified the reception's formal commencement.

The reality was that the terms of the deal had been completed and ratified by the various nations in the months and months of covert and not so covert discussions and, at times, heated debate.

The Prime Minister had made it very clear to the Prince of Wales that a deal was needed and that part of the terms were that he, as the representative of The Crown, attend the formal Trade Delegation in a ceremonial capacity. It was not easily agreed, the political commentators had made merry hell. But Great Britain needed a deal, any deal, and this was the only option they had. The Prince was reluctant but 'for the greater good goes he' was what he would always say. In private his views were a lot more forthright.

The Prime Minister had to secure a signed trade agreement at any cost and whether the electorate agreed or not right now was not important; after all the only objective with which The Prime Minster was preoccupied was political survival.

This dictatorial approach of The Prime Minister and the Number 10 political machine had certainly not been well received by Buckingham Palace. Philip Nicholson had, of course, heard the private thoughts of those that resided there and as the concessions and more onerous terms of the trade deal began to unravel and accumulate against Great Britain the more these private thoughts were giving way to grave and serious misgivings about The Prime Minister's conduct of and the direction in which the country was heading. It did not take long before LJ and Philip met and Philip's role in The Committee had been firmly agreed.

All was going to schedule. The welcome addresses were perfunctorily performed without incident and no-one noticed Sebastian as he left by one of the side doors. He and his briefcase, or at least the briefcase he was to use this evening, were alone in one of the ante rooms and gripping the handle tightly he placed the base of the case on a table and activated the fuses by turning the two identical locks on each side of the handle anti-clockwise.

It was a crudely simple plan in reality, despite what LJ claimed. There was absolutely no chance, regardless of who was in attendance at Number 10, that the Permanent Secretary to the Home Office was going to have his bags checked by the security detail. After all Sebastian was in essence their superior in both rank and title and everyone knew that he was the type of chap that would not hesitate in destroying promising or experienced careers for the slightest challenge to his authority. Sebastian had earlier walked into Number 10, through the most famous of black doors, with the arrogant air of someone that belonged in the very heart of British executive power without even as much as a hint of offering his bag for inspection.

Sebastian had to concede to LJ that the choice of the briefcase was utterly brilliant. It was the standard issue and almost the required uniform for senior Civil Servants. There would probably be several dozen exactly the same there tonight, so provided that all went to plan the likelihood of anyone connecting the dots to Sebastian was as remote as the United Kingdom winning the Eurovision Song Contest.

As Sebastian collected his final thoughts he instinctively moved his hands to his bow-tie and he was aghast to realise it was not perfectly centred. He let go of the briefcase handle to adjust the wings of his shirt and to address the offending bow-tie.

As he was undertaking this painfully precise adjustment he heard the door open and close behind him. Sebastian turned and came face-to-face with Arthur Easterby. The Deputy Director for the Department of Defence was smarting after his earlier dressing down and had been the only one to react as Sebastian had scuttled away into the room they now occupied.

"What you are doing in here," Arthur growled, "looking for a waitress to grope?" Before Sebastian could reply Easterby lurched forward so that they were almost nose-to-nose and with a hushed but sinister tone he uttered, "I know all about you and Madame Verity so don't you ever try and cross me otherwise you'll be sorry … very sorry indeed".

Sebastian's immediate reaction was 'how could he possibly know that'. But what happened next made him forget how important Easterby's last comment was.

Easterby stepped back slightly and Sebastian responded in kind in order to give valuable distance between them. However by doing so the briefcase that had just been placed on the floor so Sebastian could correct his attire was left in the no-mans land separating the two gentlemen as they now engaged each other in a fierce staring competition.

It was Easterby who broke eye-contact first and before Sebastian could make a move Arthur grabbed the briefcase with an extravagant snatch. Sebastian's instinctive reaction was to drop to his knees with his hands over his head.

This caused a raucous and guttural snort from Easterby, "Jesus, Pennington. Get a grip". Sebastian carefully rose to his feet without taking his eagle-eyed attention from the briefcase that Easterby was swinging back and forth in his right hand.

"You've not got the Crown Jewels in here so don't try and tell me you're the only one who can touch your bloody bag". With that and sensing that he had restored the usual dominance in their relationship, he casually tossed the briefcase at Sebastian.

Sebastian was never a cricketer but in those nano-seconds he wished he'd paid closer attention to the catching drills he had endured at his *alma mater*.

The briefcase spun and toppled as they were not designed with aeronautics in mind and Sebastian outstretched his arms more in hope than with any confidence. Easterby's throw had not been delivered with excessive venom and with wide-eyed relief Sebastian held on, literally for dear life, and he slumped down cradling the bag as if it were a new-born baby.

Easterby laughed out loud and declared, "You really are pathetic" and with that he nonchalantly exited the room and went back to the reception.

Sebastian was covered in perspiration, his legs felt like jelly and his hands were shaking with adrenalin. He looked down at the briefcase and hoped all was OK.

It was not.

With genuine horror he saw that one of the locking mechanisms had detached itself. How that happened he didn't know; maybe it became dislodged when Easterby threw the bag or maybe he had caused it as he clasped it so tightly to his chest.

What this meant Sebastian simply couldn't know. He had been shown on several dummy bags and prototypes only how to activate the fuse system. He didn't know whether opening the bag would set the bomb off or even if it would work now. All he knew was that there were two separate charges each linked to a fuse which, in turn, were linked to the locking mechanisms on the top of the briefcase.

With only one fuse appearing to be fully attached Sebastian could only conclude that he would have to proceed as planned, after all it was still a bomb and he had been told by LJ that there was enough explosive inside to shake the very foundations of Number 10.

So with the bomb now part-activated Sebastian returned to the main auditorium with the briefcase firmly in his left hand. He had been told to keep his right hand free so he would still be able to shake hands without drawing overt attention to what he was holding in his left hand.

LJ caught sight of a rather perturbed looking Sebastian as he gulped down a glass of apple juice. Draining his drink in one gulp Sebastian took hold of a fresh full glass and made a move back into the gathering.

Sebastian was called to join a conversation and as one of the delegates held out his right hand, Sebastian realised his mistake. With one hand gripping his briefcase and the other delicately holding a flute of pressed apple juice he had no immediate way of responding to the traditional greeting.

Sebastian momentarily recoiled and threw his drink down his gullet like a rugby-player on a night-out and as his right hand descended from his mouth he was able, in one smooth motion, to sneak the glass onto a passing waitress's tray. It all took a matter of seconds but LJ, who had noticed that Sebastian had literally got his hands full, credited him with his deftness of touch and especially for the perfectly delivered Arabic pronunciation of "A pleasure to meet you" as he warmly shook the outstretched hand.

LJ turned his attention away from Sebastian and made for The Prime Minister who he showered with praise for a 'fabulous deal well negotiated'; after all it's easier to stab someone in the back when you are standing behind them.

The early bonhomie was dissipating and The Prime Minister could sense it.

As there were so many signatories to the final Trade Agreement it was suggested and agreed by Number 10's Press Office that the actual event of signing and the required media opportunities that came with it would be best suited to the Cabinet Room.

It was not a widely popular choice given that the seats around the boat-shaped table are reserved and allocated for Cabinet members. However, The Prime Minister dictated that for once pomp and circumstance could be relaxed; after all the Trade Deal was more important than protecting the pretentious entitlement of members of the Cabinet.

The seating plan had, as with all similar occasions, been pre-negotiated and eventually agreed. Amazingly there had been a sticking point over why The Prime Minister was the only person who was allowed to have arms to their chair. After numerous hours of debate, tradition was allowed to survive. But it had taken The Prime Minister's dogmatic insistence on that entitlement to persuade the delegates to relent.

It was widely considered in the smoke-filled corridors of power afterwards that if The Prime Minister had shown the same level of tenacity over a chair as to the negotiations over Brexit or the Trade Deal itself, then the UK would not be lurching towards the disaster to which it was ultimately heading.

By oral decree from Sir William, those with the authority and permission to attend the formal signing of the Trade Deal were invited to make their way to the Cabinet Room.

There then followed the 'rush hour shuffle' which was one of the less popular methods of traversing London as delegates, representatives and authorised persons made their way slowly to the Cabinet Room.

Sebastian was in the centre of the slow moving herd of bodies and LJ could see the briefcase held tightly in his left hand. MacStones was there too, as was Sam. LJ had not been part of the selected group – he could have been if he had asked, as the sale of military hardware was one of the cornerstones of the Trade Deal, but he declined by deferentially stating that "there were others that were more needed in the room than I".

The Prime Minister had approved and the Downing Street media team rightly concluded that they didn't think it was sensible at this stage to highlight the military details of the Trade Deal by having LJ in the photographs and video clips. The country would find out all too soon that The Prime Minister had sold off most of the nation's military hardware in order to secure a short-term political victory.

Those guests that were left behind drew together sharing the same insincere stories of 'I was invited in but someone has to keep the cogs turning'. Sir William also stayed in the Pillared State Drawing Room to supervise the reception's effective continuation, and he did so by expertly engaging the Prince of Wales and Philip Nicholson in a substantive conversation about a certain Persian carpet.

After a painful minute or so of forced interaction the Prince of Wales and Nicholson departed and headed swiftly away with little fanfare. The ceremonial 'glad-handing' had been performed and at Philip's insistence it was important that the Royal Family were not seen conducting or leading matters. It was after all The Prime Minister's deal and moment to be centre stage. Departing Downing Street, both were back at Clarence House and in Philip's mind were out of harm's way.

LJ headed away from the windows and intently engaged a youngish looking gentlemen from the Middle East in conversation about his successes as a front-line commander. After all he didn't want to take any unnecessary risks of being anywhere near a lot of glass when the bomb exploded.

MacStones had pre-planned her moment to slip away – she had no need to as it was customary that the Attorney General didn't attend Cabinet meetings. She therefore set the alarm on her mobile phone to its ring tone and knowing that she could depend on Sir William's perfect punctuality she was able to step from the procession, holding her phone out in a gracious attempt at an apology.

Sam was far less cute as she opted for the obvious classic of needing an urgent comfort break after too much apple juice.

The Committee of seven had one-by-one left Sebastian alone and he suddenly felt it. His back was still sticky from his earlier 'sweat-shower' with Easterby and he began to feel very nervous as he approached the entrance to the Cabinet Room.

Of all people to be stood next to, Easterby turned to his right and whispered some foul obscenity in Sebastian's direction. As he did so he waved his right hand which was carrying the exact same type of briefcase as Sebastian and in a louder voice Easterby said, "We are both briefcase wankers today!"

It was an attempt at levity and almost solidarity but Sebastian's mind was not paying any attention at all. He did, however, raise a flicker of a smile at Easterby's reference to 'The Inbetweeners'.

Sebastian politely ushered Easterby ahead of him as they both entered the Cabinet Room and passed between the giant Corinthian columns. As they did so Sebastian could not help but marvel at the room's splendour and the fabulous array of books in the cases which, since 1931, had been added to by almost all those vacating their Cabinet positions.

It would be a shame to destroy such history but as LJ had shrewdly observed it was going to be necessary to destroy history to build a better future. This comment was a little too like one of those god-awful Facebook posts; even for Sebastian's taste. But he acknowledged the point LJ was making.

Sebastian counted at least fifteen identical briefcases to his and as he approached the only chair with arms to it he leant over the table to make sure that the documents and copies of the final Trade Deal were immaculately centred. As he stepped away he gently nudged the briefcase with his sparkling Oxford shoes so it nestled neatly upright against one of the many solid oak legs that were required to support the giant table that had been in place in the Cabinet Room since the bygone era of Gladstone.

Sebastian made his way carefully and without drawing attention to himself back to the pillars at the entrance to the room. As he did so he was able to avoid being the centre of attention as The Prime Minister and the leaders of the Middle East delegation entered and began to make their way to their allotted seats.

Sir William's perfect punctuality was all that stood in The Committee's way now.

Sebastian was now just awaiting the notification that he was required out of the Cabinet Room.

Moments passed.

Sebastian checked his watch for the umpteenth time that minute.

Moments more passed.

Sebastian was now sweating profusely. He could feel his dinner suit jacket sticking to his back. He was so on edge he even forgot to fiddle with his bow-tie.

In frantically scanning the room he realised that the Chancellor of the Exchequer was not present. "Where was he?" screamed Sebastian in his head. LJ had made it clear that the Chancellor had to suffer the same fate.

What could he do? The briefcase was now obscured by the legs of people and chairs. Sensing a terrible stomach-wrenching flash of panic Sebastian made a move towards a more panoramic view of the Cabinet Room in case one of the columns had restricted his view of the Chancellor.

As he began to shuffle forward he felt a dutiful pat on his right shoulder.

Sebastian turned around and stared into the vacuous face of his immediate subordinate who carefully and quietly mentioned that there was an urgent message waiting for him outside from a member of New Scotland Yard.

This was the pre-arranged signal for Sebastian to vacate the Cabinet Room as quickly as he could and given Sir William and LJ's attention to punctuality and detail, Sebastian had one choice; Leave or Remain. It was not a difficult choice to make in the circumstances.

Sebastian beckoned his junior towards him and firmly pulled him close so he could whisper into his ear as they stepped in unison from the room. This instruction had been dictated to him by LJ so if anyone bothered to take any notice it would appear that there was a private conversation that needed to be had and, with the mass of bodies crammed into the Cabinet Room, it was no place at all for a discreet conflab.

As Sebastian left, the doors to the Cabinet Room closed immediately behind him almost catching the heel of his trailing foot. He left his companion in his wake as he headed back to the Pillared State Drawing Room and LJ. He had been told countless times not to engage any of the other Committee members in conversation unless he absolutely had to. Sebastian felt he had no choice as there was no time left before …

He wasn't able to finish his thoughts as he came face-to-face with LJ.

Not knowing precisely what to say Sebastian attempted to convey the fact that the Chancellor of the Exchequer was not in the Cabinet Room through code words.

"Number 11 didn't make the squad". Sebastian uttered this statement with neither confidence nor poise.

Code words will only ever be effectively communicated if the participants to the conversation know the code.

LJ's face was a mixture of anger and confusion. The raised eyebrows and curling mouth conveyed to Sebastian that his attempted clandestine message had failed.

Leaning forward he tried again and this time he added greater emphasis to the first two words "N u m b e r 1 1 didn't make the squad".

LJ now understood.

Number 11 was a not so cryptic reference to the Chancellor of the Exchequer's Downing Street address. The last four words were now clear.

LJ, sensing that the conversation needed to end, calculated quickly in his head what the possible consequences could be for The Committee and their great endeavour. He had noticed that Sebastian was carrying nothing in his left hand so there was little that could be done. After all LJ rationalised it was better to take the head than nothing at all.

He stepped aloofly away from Sebastian in order to try and give the perception that their less than ten second exchange was nothing more than pleasantries.

LJ merely whispered, "Leave it."

Sebastian on hearing "Leave it" hoped that was not going to be the ultimate outcome.

There were now only moments until the briefcase bomb detonated killing The Prime Minister and no doubt countless others. The morality of the action The Committee had decided to take had caused all of them, even LJ, sleepless nights. But coldly and perhaps even cruelly, the conclusion was reached that in order to save the future of millions there was a price that a few had to pay.

Sebastian had to be away, not only out of the building but of Downing Street altogether before the bomb exploded, otherwise he would be undoubtedly caught in the security lockdown thereby being unable to lead the activation of *Gloriana*.

He headed for the famous Number 10 door, which, he often highlighted to himself, is not as recognisable from the other side. Sebastian was out and back with Jonathan who was waiting in attendance parked out of the way along with the other government vehicles. As Sebastian exited and before his Oxford shoes had hit the pavement, Jonathan and the Jaguar were in motion.

Sebastian opened the door himself and seemed to be in a rush so Jonathan, who understood his charge, deliberately said nothing as he drove the hundred yards or so to the security gates at the top of Downing Street. No-one, not even the hordes of press from around the world, seemed that interested in the departing car. The metal railing barriers were opened without so much more than passing indifference as everyone's interests and attention were focused on the momentous events taking place in the Cabinet Room.

How right all those people were.

The Jaguar turned right and the gates were closed firmly and securely behind the car and Jonathan heard from the rear seats an audible exhaling of breath. He looked into his mirror and saw Sebastian tugging at his bow tie and unbuttoning his top shirt button. Something big must have happened for him to do that thought Jonathan. It was not something that had happened but actually something that was about to happen.

The bomb exploded right on schedule.

The eruption inside the Cabinet Room was a destructive cacophony of shattering wood, glass and bones.

Nano-seconds later alarms and sirens were sounding all through the entirety of Downing Street.

Then came the screams.

People were strewn all over the Cabinet Room and more were littered half in and half out of the doors in the far corner.

The air inside was pea-soup thick with silica dust, smoke and tiny scorched fragments of paper which was all that was left of the Trade Agreement.

Bodies were writhing in agony and some were missing limbs.

There were also a small number of motionless figures.

Security Services were the first into the once ornate room followed almost immediately by the first of several paramedics.

This was no accident, no gas leak and no unexpected building collapse. Armed police came at speed from every angle and they seemed to fill every spare inch of space, effectively sealing off the Cabinet Room in a protective wall of tinted glasses and Kevlar.

LJ, Sam, MacStones and Sir William were rocked; of course they were. It's not every day a bomb explodes at Number 10 Downing Street. No matter how many times LJ had been in conflict situations before, the immediate second or so after any detonation was always greeted with relief. Today was no different.

The other three conspirators still present did not have LJ's experience and despite what had been discussed and debated hours before at New Scotland Yard all of them were ashen faced and wide-eyed with shock and terror.

LJ noted that these reactions were actually a good thing but only half a minute or so may have passed since the bomb exploded so no-one was really paying any real attention in their direction.

Sebastian was already in contact through secure lines of communication with the Deputy Prime Minister. Security officials had surrounded his office, he began to feel suffocated.

Initial reports were already flooding over Sebastian's desk.

Television and radio programmes were being interrupted with the breaking news that an explosion had occurred at Number 10.

Social media platforms were inter-sharing a meme of an incredibly obese man getting himself stuck in a revolving door.

It had only been a matter of a couple of minutes since the detonation.

It was the BBC who first posed the question of whether The Prime Minister had been injured.

Ten minutes had now passed and no-one outside of Number 10 had much idea of anything at all.

Sebastian was clear in his direction and orders. He was the Permanent Secretary to the Home Office and responsible for security and law and order throughout the country so he had to act. Those that were around him had to listen and do as they were told.

"I am invoking *Gloriana*," he declared with a firm and authoritative tone.

"As of right now, right this minute we are the British Government". He said 'we are' but he meant 'I am'.

"So we have to react and continue to govern. We don't even know what we are looking at but one thing for certain is that The Prime Minister was at Number 10 when whatever happened took place so right now the nation needs a leader to talk to them and to reassure them".

Sebastian looked at the nodding dogs in front of him and realised that they were happy to be led and in all reality would have agreed to anything he proposed.

"*Gloriana* is therefore put into immediate and total effect. The Deputy Prime Minister is now on his way directly here".

There was shuffling of feet at this last sentence and the nodding heads were all of a sudden avoiding direct eye-contact.

"Nobody knows what has happened but with the reports that I have here" he grabbed a stack of TOP SECRET memos from the nearby table and roughly scrunched them as he waved the paper like a modern day Neville Chamberlain, "they tell me that the country is without an active leader".

With that heads rose and began to nod again.

Turning to a face he recognised but not a name he could recall, Sebastian commanded, "I need copies of *Gloriana* to be immediately sent to the following departments". As he finished speaking he scattered a handful of neon-yellow post-it notes into the general direction of whom he had just addressed.

Sebastian, rightly sensing that he had full control of the room, pushed on. "*Gloriana* sets out that in the immediate aftermath of an attack no decisions are to be taken at any level of Government without prior approval of this office," his knuckles crashed down on the wooden desk as he spoke but before he could continue a voice came from the back of the room, "how do we know it was an attack?"

In the circumstances it was a fair question.

Sebastian's retort was not so fair.

"Well it is clearly not a children's party is it?" as he waved his manicured hand towards the television screen that was emitting horrific scenes of utter chaos and destruction in Downing Street.

The rolling banner said it all.

'BREAKING NEWS - Bomb blast at Downing Street – unknown casualties'

These words were repeated on a continuous loop below the images of a devastated Number 10.

Sebastian concluded, "In the absence of factual confirmation to the contrary, *Gloriana* has to be activated and adhered to".

As the bulletin kept its looping cycle it was obvious to all that Sebastian was correct and *Gloriana* needed to be initiated.

The television cameras pointed at Number 10 were broadcasting images of chaos and destruction yet inside, despite the panic, shock and noise, the medical and security teams were taking expert control and acting in a clear, calm and professional way.

The Cabinet Room had been secured and swept for secondary devices whilst fearless medics were treating the casualties.

The several lifeless bodies had been covered with jackets, table cloths or curtains. Many others were receiving life-saving treatment.

There was no sign of The Prime Minister.

LJ was directing some of his fellow service men and women.

Sam was conducting a huddled throng of the shocked and the despairing.

MacStones was desperately trying to convey a calm demeanour in the face of the destruction before her.

Sir William was collating a list of those that had been in the Cabinet Room when the bomb went off and cross-referencing that against those that had been able to declare themselves physically uninjured. This list was far shorter than he expected and it would have been shorter still if it addressed those that had been left mentally unscathed.

Clive Ferringsly's afternoon of Malbec and idle chit-chat had been interrupted with the news of the explosion as it spilled into the minds of the patrons in the public house from the news reports and the frantic scramble of people running in and out. Clive did his best to look surprised but after the lion's share of two bottles of red wine he was more intoxicated than he thought. He was feeling very tipsy and quite light-headed.

Throughout the entire country, shock and anger took over as social media began to express the views of the nation.

Initial reports, predominately based on the reports of Sir William, had the death toll at seven: Two senior aides to The Prime Minister, four from the Middle East delegation and one high-ranking Civil Servant.

LJ's first and immediate reaction to the tally was of surprise as the bomb was powerful enough to have inflicted far more carnage than that. What was clear to him though, was that whatever the final number would be it had to include the name of The Prime Minister.

Lost in his thoughts he barely noticed those representatives and delegates from the Middle East that had huddled together and were being addressed by members of the police and security forces who were failing in their attempts to prevent their mass exodus.

All was going to plan concluded LJ.

Gloriana was fully underway and being directed by Sebastian.

LJ had predicted that the media outlets would inadvertently aide their great endeavour by heightening the hysteria with their constant coverage and persistent speculation. The question that was now dominating every screen, tablet and electronic device was "Where was The Prime Minister?"

The Deputy Prime Minister strode purposely towards Sebastian with the air of a person who had arrived to lead.

"Up-to-date status report," he commanded.

Sebastian offered his summation with confidence "As of 20:18 this evening we have seven confirmed dead and the Government has been placed under the immediate and exclusive authority of *Gloriana* until further notice". With a hefty pause he followed with deliberately less emphasis, "which stipulates that you are now the *de facto* Prime Minister".

A hush enveloped Sebastian's office as these words were digested by those present.

It was unclear whether it was silence for effect that came next or silence because no-one had anything to say.

"Firstly I want direct lines to the leaders of France, Germany and the USA in order that I can reassure our primary allies that Britain is not rudderless and heading for the cliff edge." The mixed analogy was ignored as telephones were snatched and numbers punched as quickly as possible like contestants on a game show.

"I have Berlin" came the triumphant voice of the winner of 'fastest finger first'.

The receiver was taken without as much as a thank you and Sebastian authoritatively declared, "Can we have the room". Moments later the two men stood together in the midst of pandemonium and smiled at each other.

"Herr Chancellor, I wanted to make contact with you first to reassure you that Britain stands strong and stable despite this barbaric attack on our way of life and values".

Sebastian was not able to accurately hear what was said in reply but he winced at what he heard next.

"Let me assure you Herr Chancellor that we will be victorious in the unrelenting quest for those responsible but in the meantime I, on behalf of us all here, urge you to provide all of Germany's support and assistance in the coming hours and days".

Two red lights were flickering and as the call with Germany ended each 'call waiting' signal was pressed and similar conversations occurred with the Presidents of France and the USA.

Sebastian blushed as all three conversations opened with 'I wanted to make contact with you first'.

Sam was now undertaking complex discussions about the possible effects the explosion would have on Great Britain's immediate economy and its future. From her point of view these were going well and the seeds of concern were being expertly sown for others to harvest. Speculation that the surviving members of the Middle East delegation were adamant they were to depart never to return fuelled the conversations that needed to occur for The Committee and their great endeavour to succeed.

Sir William and MacStones were similarly busy.

Philip Nicholson was sat in uncomfortable silence at Clarence House with the Prince of Wales who was now under increased security.

Clive Ferringsly felt a bit better so he had moved on to single-malt whiskies.

LJ's mind was frantically assessing the situation and events going on around him.

As planned for, *Gloriana* would now be taking hold of the requisite branches of government and the Deputy Prime Minister would be making the pre-prescribed calls setting the tone for the future policy of Remaining within the EU.

The most critical aspect of everything he had calculated was still unknown to him and that was whether The Prime Minister had been killed.

LJ moved with a deliberate stride as he noticed two paramedics moving quickly to the Cabinet Room and what caught LJ's attention was that they did not appear to be focusing on the carnage around them but were intent on reaching their objective; whatever that might be.

LJ stepped in to line behind them and followed them into the devastated Cabinet Room and out onto the terrace. As he moved through the once ornate chamber his shoes crunched on the debris beneath his feet.

Sebastian was in his element and enjoying the power and purpose placed upon him. He was feeling king-like as he wielded his authority across the country dictating to all he spoke to in a tone and fashion that could not be questioned. After all he was only following the written instructions of *Gloriana*.

It was nothing more than a brutal *coup d'état* and, while others would claim to be the new king, Sebastian was maniacally spewing forth instructions, commands and directives in a manner not dissimilar to the armchair football fanatic.

The Deputy Prime Minister had finished his call sheets having spoken to and reassured most of the EU and NATO leaders that Britain, despite the obvious atrocity, had a dependable captain at the helm capable of steering the nation through this rocky terrain and uncharted waters. Sebastian was again not overly content with yet further contradictory analogies but the Deputy Prime Minister announced that as Parliament had been waiting in session in order to immediately vote on the signed Trade Deal he was now actually able to address them as its *de facto* leader.

This was it; this was the entire 'ball game'. Parliament had essentially been convened to hear the first address of the new Prime Minister.

Sebastian and the next leader of the nation left for the Palace of Westminster and were ushered through that most famous of old buildings with a sombre reverence reserved for state funerals.

Sebastian followed in step to the rhythmic beat of the two sets of heels which announced their arrival through the corridors of power like battle drums of olde.

Through the Central Lobby they proceeded but then Sebastian held back and stopped so he could watch the Deputy Prime Minister carry on forward into the Members' Lobby and into the Commons Chamber with those iconic green benches.

Sam and MacStones had migrated to opposite ends of the entrance hall to Number 10; this was not on purpose it just seemed to happen that way.

MacStones was deeply engaged in a heated debate over the legal position regarding the Trade Agreement as there seemed to be some confusion about whether it had been formally signed or not. One of the debaters was advancing the point that signed or unsigned the actual deal had been agreed months ago during those turgid and protracted negotiations. Another debater identified the fact that legally binding or not where were their Middle Eastern counterparts now? "On the first plane outta here," he quipped mimicking the universal hitch-hiking hand-gesture as he spoke.

MacStones had little left to do as she spoon-fed to her underlings the seeds of doubt over the future of the Trade Agreement and she expertly brought the conversation back to Brexit. "We don't know what is going to happen next but with the only viable trade deal literally up in smoke we are going to have to carefully look into what can be done about reversing Article 50."

She didn't wait for a response as she directed, "Today is the day to keep a level head and we are doing our job by presenting whoever is in charge tomorrow with every option available. I want position papers on my desk and ready for dissemination by 0600 and I want the lawyers who advise the President of the European Council on the phone before they even get to sit down tomorrow morning …" with a pause she added, "provided we get out of here sometime soon". The collective response was merely exhausted nods of agreement.

Sam had noticed MacStones and MacStones had of course noticed Sam but neither offered either smile or gesture of affection despite the death and pain that surrounded them.

Sam was listening intently to three of her colleagues debating the finer points of the suggestions she had just laid out to them. "There is no conceivable way that the economy can exist without a major trade pact or the EU trading block" squealed one. "Well what choice is there now," came the reply. The third was playing interactive tennis as his head turned left then right, left and then right as the two others rallied back and forth with their arguments but neither won the decisive point. It was Sam who secured 'Game, Set and Match' but it was an unfairly balanced contest given that she had already been discussing the 'how do we Remain' issue with her European economic colleagues.

"It might be that the long term economic interests of the UK are going to be best served if we look at all scenarios including Remaining in the EU".

Three sets of eyes gazed upon her. Sam exuded calmness as she spoke.

"We have no idea of what is going to happen next and our job is to present all sides of the argument, so I want to see detailed forecasts from all angles and that includes Remaining".

Before any could respond Sir William joined the gang of four, "Apologies for interrupting but I understand that the Deputy Prime Minister is about to address Parliament".

LJ was still standing in the Cabinet Room trying to peer through the shattered window frames into the terrace outside. He was aware that he began to sense a dreadful feeling in his stomach. Whilst craning his neck he saw a group of security officials heading away from the building where he stood.

The Deputy Prime Minister had addressed Parliament before in an official capacity, having answered Prime Minister's Questions on a handful of occasions.

This was an entirely different situation though and as he approached the Dispatch Box the entire chamber rose to its feet and a thunderous and quite spontaneous applause echoed and bounced from all sides. Every Member was standing and applauding, the gallery was full and dozens of heads were skewed at all vantage points in order that they may witness what was taking place.

It was going so well he thought and the ovation was doing a marvellous job of drowning out his rapidly beating heart.

The speech that had been carefully pre-prepared was placed delicately on the gold coloured lectern. His hands, that were thankfully not visibly shaking too much, were placed with great care on either side.

The clapping continued.

He raised his right hand and Members began to return to their seats. Those that were stood in the aisles shuffled their feet as they came together like wet sand in a bucket.

"Today," began the speech, "is an occasion that will never be forgotten or forgiven in the history …" Shouts of approval masked the next few words.

Sebastian was outside and was part of a melee of officials and Civil Servants standing in silence as they tried to overhear what was being announced a few feet in front of them.

Sebastian was in a unique position though as he already knew what was going to be said but he was conscious that he needed to be seen to be attentively listening.

He was stood shoulder to shoulder with a chap from the Department from Works and Pensions who whispered into his ear.

"I just wanted to offer my condolences, Mr Pennington".

Sebastian was sure his heart stopped

"What?" was all he could say in reply.

"I know you knew him well so I …"

"What?" interrupted Sebastian.

"Easterby … you knew him well didn't you?"

With more urgency and inflection than the two times before Sebastian pronounced, "What?"

"Easterby … he was killed earlier".

Sebastian's legs wobbled, not in grief but in relief.

"Errrrrr, yes I did ... Thank you … he was a good … friend".

Sebastian was elated and struggled to conceal his utter joy at the news. He undid his second top button of his dress shirt and sucked in a lung full of sweet air. He exhaled deeply with his head tilted back to the ceiling and briefly closed his eyes and thought to himself "Could this day get any better?"

Inside the House of Commons the Deputy Prime Minister was on sparkling form and it seemed to him that every sentence he uttered was met with rapturous acclaim.

It was now the part of the speech where he would address Parliament and the nation with regards to the future of Brexit and whether or not in the wake of such disaster a revisionist approach should be adopted.

There was no secret at all in his personal standpoint. He was one of the primary advocates of the Remain Team within the Government. He had worked closely with the EU at all levels and with Clive Ferringsly who had headed up the legal team to challenge the Brexit bill even after the Referendum.

It was political expediency on behalf of The Prime Minister who nominated him as Deputy. After all, Brexit was not a party political issue. All the major parties were riven with division over it and the make-up of the House of Commons, which used to be readily discernible by colour, was now a melting pot of distrust and inter-party factions.

It was a simple fact of Brexit that even die-hard left wingers would collaborate with staunch Conservatives on this issue and would even be seen grouped together in whispered conversations whereas, on every other political subject, they would not even wish to be in the same room as each other.

Brexit had changed British politics forever, only time would tell if it would be for the better.

The fracturing of the established 'left/right' political battle lines were not as clear cut as just those that were Remain or Leave. There were also seemingly endless debates over hard or soft Brexit or deal or no deal Brexit and every facet and permutation had its own set of advocates and dissenters.

At the very centre of this spider's web of political machinations was The Prime Minister.

"There are undoubtedly some complex decisions that need to be carefully considered and ruminated on over the course of the coming hours and days and one of these, given the barbaric events of earlier this evening, is the continued policy of Leaving the European Union".

Never had the House of Commons been so quiet.

The Deputy Prime Minister quickly scanned the opposition rows in front of him. In the immediate seconds after his last sentence he stared ahead and saw that more mouths had dropped open before him than he could easily count.

Then began the cheers.

"Hear, hear". "Hear, hear". "Hear, hear," was bellowed from all corners of the chamber.

The acclamation seemed to get louder and louder but in actual fact it only seemed that way as it was amalgamated with cries of "Shame". "Shame". "Shame".

The Speaker of the House could not control this unruly rabble. The red dividing lines that were two swords width apart could not abate the vitriol that was being hurled. The fracas was not confined to either side of the House as scuffles broke out in every direction. Order Papers were being used as makeshift batons.

"Order ... ORDER," bellowed the Speaker as he saw utter chaos erupting before his very eyes. The scenes being broadcast around the world looked nothing short of football hooligans running amok on the terraces in the 1980s.

The Deputy Prime Minister was pleading for calm but his best efforts were drowned out by the sheer decibel level of the disharmony around him.

The Speaker was hoarse from his desperate attempts to maintain order.

Then as if the entire Chamber had passed into the eye of the storm, serenity washed over everyone and everything. The only movement was the fluttering down of strewn pages of the Order Papers.

The Deputy Prime Minister looked horrified as his mouth dropped open like a drawbridge. The Speaker cleared his throat with a hefty cough and went to speak but before he could every single Member of Parliament, with the exception of one, began cheering and hollering as if Winston Churchill himself had entered.

In walked The Prime Minister, visibly shaken and moving with a very pronounced limp but moving nevertheless and moving with purpose.

The adulation got louder and the make-shift batons that were weapons a few moments earlier were now being used to beat the green pews as if they were signal drums welcoming home a victorious conqueror.

The Deputy Prime Minister began to clap as loudly and forcefully as he could. He even tried to feign delight in his face but his facial expression showed a mixture of rage and fear.

The Prime Minister reached the Dispatch Box to rapturous acclaim.

The Speaker by summoning his most barbaric yawp from the very depths of his stomach screamed, "The Prime Minister!"

The applause lasted for over five and a half minutes and despite The Prime Minister's appeal for silence none was forthcoming. Even the Speaker was lost in this triumphant moment as he beamed down from his chair made of the finest Australian black beanwood.

Finally with aching arms and sore hands the din quietened to an eventual silence.

The Prime Minister turned to the nation's Deputy and with a vengeful tone quietly remarked, "If you don't mind, I'll take it from here".

The Deputy Prime Minister had no choice but to vacate the floor and he slumped down onto the front bench. There was not sufficient room however for his ample backside so, embarrassingly, he sat perched on one cheek with the other tilted against the Home Secretary.

The Prime Minister's voice was audibly shaken but the events of the earlier hours were recounted to the dumb-struck House and the disbelieving World.

Every media outlet was 'live' as regular TV shows were interrupted; much to the annoyance of devotees of soap operas, but the greatest drama was actually unfolding in real life with no scripts and no re-takes but plenty of plots.

This time the rolling news banner was able to definitively declare 'Prime Minister survives bomb blast'.

Sebastian was sweating so profusely that he looked like he had just stepped out of the shower. He turned and fought his way through the massed bodies that were competing to catch a glimpse of events in the House. He broke free and rushed towards the nearest exits.

He hadn't noticed that he had started to run; he didn't even hear the shouts of stop and he most certainly didn't hear the bullet that struck him in the chest. He felt it though as he was propelled forward and downwards to the marble floor.

There were no onlookers that noticed given the happenings elsewhere and security officials encircled the prostrate Sebastian in seconds and spirited him away down St Stephen's Hall and into the adjoining Cloister Court.

Sebastian was alive but barely.

An armed policemen shouted, "Let's have a proper look at this ..." His words were lost in his mouth as he stared down into the despairing eyes of the Permanent Secretary to the Home Office, the man who was responsible for the nation's security and law order.

"You fuckin' prick, Paul," as he turned to the marksman, "you've just shot our boss".

Paul sank to his knees. "He was running around lookin' like a nutter just minutes after someone blew the shit out of Number 10 so what was I meant to do ...? And I warned him three times to stop," he added for good measure.

"Well you better keep praying he makes it," was the reply.

Paul was hunched over now trying to frantically help in the medical treatment being urgently administered to

Sebastian and he was sure he overheard his victim mumble "Glory".

LJ was still in Number 10 and he was back in the Pillared State Drawing Room trying to join in the celebrations but he didn't share the same sense of relief as everyone else. He forced himself to repeat the "it's a miracle" line but he failed to say it with equal sentiment.

He stood watching The Prime Minister addressing Parliament not knowing how that could be physically occurring. He turned with his mind muddled with too many questions that all seemed to start with either 'Why?' or 'How?'.

He walked carefully back to the Cabinet Room and was surprised to see the sentries on guard. His mind was elsewhere otherwise the fact that these soldiers were not *in situ* a few minutes ago would not have been overlooked.

As he passed by them, he caught the taller one's eyes and as he did so the guard stood to attention with a stiffness that only those that had been in military possessed. "Good evening, Sir," came the crisp deep voice. LJ stopped and turned to face this imposing figure. "Served under you in Bosnia, Sir and pleased to see you're in charge here". LJ smiled weakly back as he entered the Cabinet Room.

"Give the bastards hell, Sir".

LJ moved deeper into the bomb-ravaged shell of a room thinking to himself "I tried … I really tried".

In the centre of the room was the Cabinet table. LJ was aghast and more than a little confused to see that it was still identifiable as a table. It was blackened and portions were missing from the side facing LJ but it was most definitely still a table. LJ could not figure out how that was even possible.

"It's a miracle isn't it" came a voice over LJ's left shoulder. He turned to face The Chancellor of the Exchequer who continued, "Apparently from what I've been told the explosion occurred up against one of those solid wooden legs which softened the blast".

LJ nodded along.

"It is just so fortunate for The PM that there was some last minute haggling over places around the table".

"Uh-huh," was all that LJ could muster.

The Chancellor continued to explain that the shift in seating arrangements meant that The PM was moved away from the epicentre of the immediate blast area.

"But how do you know that The Prime Minister was the target and not anyone else?" commented LJ.

"Well who else could it be," came the immediate retort. "The Middle East delegation could have been targeted anytime and anywhere and frankly the immediate incidents following the blast suggest that it was us that was the objective and not them".

LJ felt uncomfortable by the use of 'us' and 'them'.

"What incidents?" he tried to be casual and curious as he spoke.

"Look here, LJ," the Chancellor squeezed LJ's left wrist, "too much went on too quickly and The PM was not even confirmed dead and yet ... and yet". The Chancellor stopped abruptly and gazed towards the outside terrace.

"Put it this way, it's starting to look like a failed coup and The PM and I were talking only half an hour or so ago just out there," he gesticulated outside, "that it all seemed a little too coincidental".

LJ could feel the need to shuffle his feet but he held his stance knowing that the Chancellor was getting a little too close for comfort.

"We are going to want to catch every single one of those bastards and we want you to do it for us LJ".

LJ reacted well, given the circumstances.

"I'll do whatever it takes of course. But right now there is little to go on until a full inspection has occurred".

"No need for that my *dear* friend"

With that deliberate enunciated 'dear', LJ couldn't fight the urge to move anymore. He shuffled his bearing from side-to-side.

"What do you mean? – it's a hell of task that needs to be done as quickly as possible but most importantly it has to be done right".

"I fully agree with you" replied the Chancellor. "It's a great endeavour".

LJ moved quickly for the terrace but was surrounded and man-handled to the floor by half a dozen burly guards and the two soldiers he had only recently passed by. He was hauled to his feet and presented to members of MI5 who appeared from the dusty confines of the room's corners.

"It was planned with military precision LJ but you relied on too many civilians".

Those words never left the forefront of LJ's mind for the rest of his mortal days which, as it turned out, were not that many in number.

He was interrogated, deprived of sleep and water but he never spoke again to anyone about anything.

LJ was desperate to know how he had been found out and how his plan had failed but he refused to ask. The Chancellor's carefully chosen words had provided LJ with enough information for him to safely conclude that either someone had betrayed him or that their secret meetings had somehow been recorded or monitored.

It was irrelevant as his plan had failed.

Sebastian was breathing and in a lot of excruciating pain. He was in and out of consciousness but he was alive - unlike seven other people.

He woke briefly to a bright white room. His eyes closed and he fell back into a deep stupor.

When he finally wrestled himself awake he found that he couldn't move his right arm - there was something cold against his skin. He tried to move his hand up to his eyes and he heard a metallic jangle. With a huge exertion given the pain in the centre of his chest, he looked down to see his right hand had been handcuffed to the side rail of his bed.

Sebastian slumped backwards in agony; his head was fuzzy and his memory shaken but as he peered through his heavy eyes he glimpsed bodies moving towards him. His eyes closed and he fell back asleep.

Clive Ferringsly died that very evening of a massive heart-attack. All the team at Hartington Chambers were utterly shocked having had the pleasure of his spontaneous visit earlier that afternoon. He had died in the snug bar where the staff could not recall how many whiskies he had imbibed in addition to a hefty dose of red wine. Some concluded that his big heart had given way in the euphoric scenes as The Prime Minister had gloriously entered the House of Commons. That was a close assessment but it was not entirely accurate.

Sam and MacStones had heard the commotion in the Cabinet Room as LJ had been led away. Sam saw the immediate aftermath and she caught the eyes of the Chancellor as he approached her.

"Bastard," was all he said as he purposefully walked by.

MacStones went to Sam having witnessed this brief exchange and they hugged tightly and, as they finally released each other, Sir William joined them.

"LJ has been taken," was all he said.

LJ was sitting in a stress position against the wall of a Private Secretary's office in Number 10 with nothing to do but contemplate how the plan had failed.

It was clear having just been in the Cabinet Room that the bomb had not fully detonated but despite being threatened with a trial for treason LJ refused to even confirm his name.

Sebastian had become deliriously incoherent and little actual help to MI5 in their efforts to piece together that day's tumultuous events.

"Tell me about *Gloriana*".

"We know Brigadier General Xavier Llewellyn-Jones and you conspired to assassinate The Prime Minister".

"Madame Verity told us everything you boasted to her about … You really should have a little more discretion".

Sebastian was able to be raised from his reclined position the next day and the same questions were put to him.

The second time he said absolutely nothing at all but the single tear that ran from his left eye to the corner of his mouth said more than words could ever do.

Over the coming days Sebastian's health improved slightly, he had been very lucky indeed as the bullet had passed through his chest without hitting any major organs. He didn't feel lucky.

MI5 had been alerted by one of its most reliable informants; it was not her real name but Madame Verity catered for the London elite's very particular tastes. It was often politicians, government officials and industry leaders rather than the bankers, lawyers and brokers who had their own more high street forms of adult entertainment.

Sebastian had not divulged the when and the where and nor who. The target was however, so the moment the bomb exploded he was doomed. It was merely a coincidence that he was shot and it only sped up the process of him being detained. The ridiculousness of it all was that a few boastful comments and wanting to impress a Madame had led to the ultimate failure of The Committee and their great endeavour.

Sebastian didn't even make the first stage of interrogation.

It was a surprising choice that he made and he was actually proud of how calm he was about it. He just needed to recover enough for his plan to succeed.

LJ was taken to Belmarsh Prison and placed in immediate solitary confinement. LJ waited, knowing that eventually MacStones would arrive.

He didn't have to wait that long. He was shown into an empty communal area by a number of prison guards. He was roughly placed on a single plastic chair in the middle of this depressingly awful room. A number of people filed in and one of them was MacStones. He was asked time and time and time again, "Who else was involved?" "Who planted the bomb?" Even MacStones asked LJ, "Who else was part of this conspiracy?"

LJ said nothing. He sat with his hands under his bottom and out of easy eye-sight. He was rubbing his forefinger nail up and down at acute angles in order to sharpen his nail as best he could.

At the end of this pseudo-interrogation MacStones and LJ shared the tiniest of moments. LJ was sure he saw a flicker of a warm smile from her. He was vigorously and invasively searched before he was allowed to re-enter his cell but when he was back alone he continued to file his nail against the brickwork. After several hours of careful grooming and sharpening he was left with a nail just under half an inch in length but most importantly it had been sculpted and crafted into a viciously sharp point.

He knew it was going to hurt but the consequences of not doing anything would cause more harm to him than he could possibly endure. At 02:13 on the morning after The Committee tried to assassinate The Prime Minister, Brigadier General Xavier Llewellyn-Jones jabbed his sharpened nail through his Adventitia, the outermost layer of tissue of his carotid artery. He dug deep into his neck knowing that he had only seconds before he passed out. He tore at his skin and tissue like a zombie until blood was pouring out of him like water from a hosepipe.

As he knew he would, LJ passed out and he never again regained consciousness. The guard who was scheduled to undertake the morning cell inspection was so traumatised by the sight that greeted him he never worked again and spent the rest of his days a shadow of his former self.

Sebastian's exit was far less brutal but it was equally as effective.

He had been making note of the medical staff's precise comings and goings and of those on duty guarding him. He needed to save his energy as he would have to move quickly and timing was everything.

By regularly twisting his right wrist as hard as he could against the coarseness of the metal handcuff he was soon able to break the skin and as he continued a trickle of blood began to drip onto the bedsheets. He pretended to be asleep as a healthcare assistant released the shackle and exited the room looking to report to the duty nurse.

His chance had arrived and Sebastian was out of bed, his bare feet felt alive again against the medical facility's cold tiled floor. He headed straight for the closed door dragging one of the chairs with him. He tipped the chair on its legs and against the door with the back-rest under the handle.

He then turned to the window and moved with forceful purpose. With one almighty yank he pulled the roller-blinds down and off their fittings. With a further desperate grab he managed to rip off the majority of the blinds so he was left with the cord in one hand.

All of this took place in less than five seconds.

There began a thunderous rattling at the door as the handle shook like it was being treated as a snow-globe by an overactive child. Alarms began to drown out the rattling and thumps of clenched fists on wood. Sebastian ignored the commotion with the indifference of a person completely focused on their objective.

The cord was wound around his neck as tightly as it could be and he managed to climb to a standing position on top of his bed. He looped the other end of the cord over the hook that was affixed to the ceiling in case a patient needed a gurney.

By now the alarms were almost inaudible against the barrage of crash and bangs as the door was being rushed at from the outside like a tackling bag at American Football training.

Sebastian had no time for a prayer but then he was not religious. He always found it more than a little insincere for those on their death beds to suddenly find God.

Before he leapt he managed one final adjustment to what he was wearing around his neck. It was a very strange habit he had developed and he couldn't recall how it began and lost in that odd thought he leapt away from the bed.

It was not a dignified end for Sebastian and the improvised form meant it was most certainly not immediate. He slowly throttled himself to death just as the door was finally burst open.

The media reported that Sebastian Pennington and LJ had been unscrupulous anti-muslims who were intent on destroying Britain's Middle East trade negotiations. LJ's reputation was left devastated and his name was expunged from all public military records. As for Sebastian, his actions saved him from the final act of indignity in seeing that Arthur Easterby was immortalised for evermore with his name being etched into an *in memoriam* plaque that was affixed in the very centre of the reconditioned table in the Cabinet Room.

Natalie moved house. She left behind all of Sebastian's possessions that MI5 had discarded as being irrelevant to the investigation in over a dozen searches and inspections. She even left the mat by the doorstep.

The Deputy Prime Minister escaped with his life because he was simply too stupid to have been actively involved. Madame Verity could neither confirm nor deny his involvement and therefore he was allowed to graciously step down from front line politics and to retire to the country. It was not really retirement as The Prime Minister insisted on a 24 hour watch being put in place; it was more like house arrest than anything else. But the Deputy Prime Minister didn't have the gumption to take his own life. He found God though and became a student of religious studies. His faith in the divine forgiveness of the Lord sustained him for the rest of his life.

Clive Ferringsly's funeral was standing room only. The Temple Church not far from Hartington Chambers was simply not large enough to accommodate all that wanted to come and pay their respect.

MacStones was the only member of The Committee to attend and she did so in her capacity as Secretary of State for Justice. This was a distinct promotion from her role as Attorney General. It was deserved, said The Prime Minister. And MacStones was simply not the kind of person to turn down a promotion, increased authority and media attention. And a proper and genuine chair as a Cabinet member who would now meet in the newly decorated and designed Cabinet Room. It was never lost on MacStones as she sat there that she had been part of the most radical coup to take place in Britain since 1605 and yet here she was with a seat at the table. She could not help herself but to envy The Prime Minister's armed chair. "Maybe one day that chair will be mine," she thought.

Sir William was never quite sure how he had never been arrested or questioned over what he knew about

Sebastian and LJ's plan to assassinate The Prime Minister. Whilst Sebastian had been, to his and LJ's detriment and ultimately death, utterly reckless in his comments and words to Madame Verity, he had only ever mentioned LJ by name.

Sir William resigned as Cabinet Secretary with immediate effect. He claimed that his nerve had gone and no-one blamed him for that. Some of his colleagues even remarked that he never looked the same again but in reality that was actually due to the fact that Sir William was living in a constant state of trepidation that he might be arrested and tried for treason. He was never investigated and so he returned to the family business. He requested and received the role of Company Secretary but he maintained and insisted that he was still referred to as Sir William.

Sam left The Treasury with no stain at all on her service record. She was offered millions of pounds a year to join a private investment bank. She declined and instead won a Nobel Prize for Economics, twice. Or as Sam preferred to say she won back-to-back Sveriges Riksbank Prizes in Economic Sciences in Memory of Alfred Nobel. Her choice of words made it actually sound less of an achievement but she ultimately became one of the most sought after Macroeconomic lecturers of her generation.

The four Middle Eastern delegates who were killed in the explosion were given posthumous honours and the George Cross no less but that was the absolute entirety of what passed between the two parties that were within a few moments of agreeing trillions of pounds in trade deals. The Prime Minister was overheard several months after the bomb blast saying that it was the best thing that ever happened to Great Britain, but no-one really understood or questioned what was meant by that remark.

As for Brexit, The Prime Minister, with *Gloriana* deactivated, continued to negotiate the best possible terms and with new found popular support both in the House of Commons and throughout the country there was not much that could be done to challenge The Prime Minister.

Philip Nicholson never gambled again. He tried it two days or so after The Committee's attempt at murdering The Prime Minister but it did not carry the same level of excitement and 'buzz' as before. It took him a while to realise why.

Philip engineered the meeting at Clarence House without any difficultly at all. These palatial buildings were open to visitors and in his position of Master of the Royal Household it was not difficult to commandeer The Garden Room for a private gathering.

There were six occupied chairs as Philip turned away from watching the shadow on the sun dial out in the garden, so as he sat down that made seven.

With confident composure Philip opened the conversation. "Firstly, thank you all for coming. I appreciate that your collective time is invaluable so I don't intend to keep you long but I have met with you all separately over the last week or so and now is the time for us all to meet and to discuss what can be done to reverse the ruinous policy of Brexit?"

With the raising of his right hand, as if he were back at school asking permission to speak, a mild-mannered boy-ish looking man of around thirty years old responded. "It seems to me that the only viable option is direct action". Nicholson nodded and in an agreeable tone replied, "And what does direct action actually mean do you think?"

"Well … probably eradicating The Prime Minister" was the response.

Nicholson looked around the lavish surroundings and into the eyes of everyone who was attentively waiting for him to say something.

"It is the *only* way". And with that a committee was formed.

THE END

THE STORY OF VALKYRIE

Valkyrie is a 2008 movie, based on real events, starring Tom Cruise set during World War II and it depicts a conspiratorial plot to assassinate Adolf Hitler.

Cruise plays Claus Von Stauffenberg, a German Colonel, who on 20 July 1944, detonated a bomb inside Hitler's military headquarters in East Prussia in order for the army to then seize political control away from the Nazis with the ultimate aim of avoiding the impending ruinous destruction of Germany.

Operation Valkyrie was a plan designed to implement the continuation of Germany's governmental operations in the wake of general civil unrest and disorder. Von Stauffenberg and his fellow conspirators altered Valkyrie in order that, after the death of Hitler, they could effectively disarm the Nazi Party and arrest its remaining leaders and to assert jurisdiction over the major German cities.

The bomb exploded but failed to kill Hitler as he was largely shielded from its impact by a wooden table leg. Von Stauffenberg had excused himself from the military briefing and was able to depart the scene before it was locked down. Operation Valkyrie was put into immediate effect and was appearing to succeed until rumours began to be received that Hitler had in fact survived. Survived he did. And when, some hours after the explosion he addressed Germany via a radio broadcast, this effectively terminated the impact and implementation of Operation Valkyrie.

Von Stauffenberg was part of a far wider network of senior German officials, politicians and officers who were actively seeking to assassinate Hitler. However, and as history teaches us, Hitler did bring ruinous destruction upon Germany. He finally died, by committing suicide in his Berlin bunker with the Soviet Army only a few hundred metres away.

As for Von Stauffenberg, he and several other of the leading plotters were put to death by firing squad in the early hours of 21 July 1944. Several hundred more were arrested, 'tried' and executed in the coming weeks. Hitler utilised the plot against him to undergo a brutal purge throughout Germany which lead to the execution or imprisonment of tens of thousands of Germans.

Valkyrie was directed by Bryan Singer who had previously directed The Usual Suspects and X-Men and the stellar cast included Kenneth Branagh, Bill Nighy, Terence Stamp, Tom Wilkinson and Eddie Izzard.

Gloriana is the fifth title in the *Novella Nostalgia* series wherein iconic films inspire modern stories. Its theme reflects the 2008 Tom Cruise film, *Valkyrie*, wherein there is a conspiratorial plot to kill Adolf Hitler.

The *Novella Nostalgia* series have been described by many as so gripping that they can't be put down. With many five-star reviews, you should not miss out on the City Fiction's authors; Tony Drury and Oliver Richbell.

Full details of the *Novella Nostalgia* series can be found at www.cityfiction.co.uk

ABOUT THE AUTHOR

After spending over a decade as a lawyer, Oliver runs a dispute resolution consultancy that helps businesses resolve their commercial disputes through dialogue and negotiation. He is Chairman of Bedfordshire's region of *Wooden Spoon*, a charity that helps socially, mentally and physically disadvantaged children and he is also a volunteer at a local homeless outreach organisation. He lives in Bedford with his wife and daughter. Oliver has published his first solo novella *Gloriana* which is inspired by the Tom Cruise film, *Valkyrie*. Using the background of 'Brexit', *Gloriana* creates a thunderous political thriller with a mesmeric ending.

Having collaborated with Tony Drury on *Twelve Troubled Jurors*, Oliver has also written *The Courageous Witness* based on the movie *The Accused*. It will published in early 2019 as part of the Novella Nostalgia series and it also launches the character of Barrister Amanda Buckingham: there are many more legal stories to follow.

On top of all of that, Oliver is writing a novel.